# *Chocka's Story*

– BARRY KAUFMANN-WRIGHT –

FASTPRINT PUBLISHING
PETERBOROUGH, ENGLAND

CHOCKA'S STORY



ISBN 978-184426-827-6

First published 2010 by
FASTPRINT PUBLISHING
Peterborough, England.

Printed in England by
www.printondemand-worldwide.com

# *Acknowledgements*

*My wife Pat for her continued patience in my writing exploits, and for correcting my initial grammar and spelling mistakes.*

*My daughter Georgina for proof reading my scribbling.*

*Sue Roderick for also proof reading my scribbling.*

*John Paley for his superb artistry.*

*Peter and Jan Aylett for allowing us and the dogs the free access to their farm, where many of the adventures described by Chocka occurred.*

*All my family and friends for allowing their names to be used.*

# *Introduction*

This is a story of a dog that was homed by the author and his wife after she had spent some time as a stray in the small market town of Saffron Walden in north west Essex. It is known from local vet's records and from the local animal warden that she was run down by cars on the roads at least three times during her time on the streets. When she arrived with the author she was very thin, emaciated, and bruised, both physically and mentally.

She soon recovered and became one of the most affectionate, obedient, faithful, tactile, and playful dogs the author and his wife had ever owned. She had to be close to one of them all the time. She had no name when she arrived, so she was named 'Chocka'. This is her story of some of her recollections and adventures told by her to the author over the years that she has lived at 'Pandemonium'. It has been great fun writing both for Chocka and the author and we hope you enjoy the story as much as we have enjoyed writing it.

*This book is dedicated to my wife Pat*

Other books by the same author:

Running Wild

The Wildlife Man

Cassie

Jack of All Trades



All the photographs in this book are the work of the author

All the sketches are the work of John Paley

Published by Fastprint Publishing 2010

# Index of stories

# *The Early Days*

My story begins in a garden shed of a house in a town called Saffron Walden in north-west Essex, on a cold February night in 1997. I was one of 5 puppies born to our mother 'Trudy', a yellow Labrador. Our father was not known: - mum had sneaked off one night and returned pregnant.

Although we were blind we were not deaf, I could hear the cold wind blowing outside. Mum kept us close and kept us warm. We soon learnt where the food was, her warm milk was lovely. For the first few weeks I did nothing but eat and sleep, my eyes slowly opened and I could see shapes, the bright daylight coming in through the open door.

The women that lived in the house had moved out in a hurry and had abandoned mum and us to our fate. Mum had somehow managed to open the door of the shed by releasing the catch, and the swinging door would bang in the wind. The door was frightening as it would often bang shut. The noise would scare me and, being plunged into darkness. As we grew older the door would sometimes catch us as we passed through it but we learnt to miss it.

Mum would go off and find food for herself as best she could. Although she was very thin she still managed to provide us with enough milk, but it was becoming more and more of a struggle for her.

Our home was a wooden box in the shed at the end of the garden. It was cold but dry and it was home for quite a while. As my eyes began to focus, the interior of the shed became clear. In a corner stood an old broom which we soon found was great fun as we dragged it around and played with it, till the brush fell to bits.

As the weeks went on and we grew, we became more and more inquisitive and began to investigate the great wide world outside the shed, avoiding the swinging door of course. The garden was very overgrown and we had great fun chasing each other through the long grass. I was the only female and got picked on quite a bit. The games became more and more rough as the fights were more in earnest - the early teeth were very sharp - but I soon learned to give as good as I got. After a lot of running and rolling around I would go off in search of any insects to eat. Some insects had begun to appear in the undergrowth as the days lengthened and became warmer, but this was short lived as one of the other pups would leap up onto my back and bite my ears, which I did not like.

As mum's milk began to dry up we were forced to look further afield for food. Her visits to us were becoming less frequent and she was becoming very short tempered with us. Our early teeth had now been replaced by much more substantial ones. We were growing fast and becoming more adventurous. There was an open back gate to the garden that led into an alleyway with high wooden fences either side, a scary place. This led down to an even scarier place where strange loud monsters went racing past - I was to learn that these were cars and they could really hurt.

Early in the mornings we would all go off to try and find food, and to begin with we would soon return to the safety of the garden and shed. Food was hard to find and I was forced to look in litter bins which I had difficulty reaching into. Sometimes I would strike lucky but more often than not I went hungry. I was always pleased at the end of the day to return to the shed and see my brothers.

However soon after we all began to wander and scavenge for food, disaster struck! One evening I returned to the alley as usual, but on reaching the gate into the garden, I discovered that it was firmly closed. There was no sign of any of the others. I sat and waited, looking anxiously at the closed gate. Suddenly I heard voices coming from the garden, I barked loudly, again and again. The gate opened and a huge man stood there. He looked down at me and shouted loudly. The tone of his voice suggested to me that he was not happy with me - I had heard that tone before when I was trying to scrounge food around the town.

I saw a gap between his legs so I ran through them to open the gate and into the garden, desperately looking for mum and the others, but there was no sign of them. I ran up to the shed door which was firmly shut.

The man came after me and shouted at me and tried to kick me, I just managed to dodge the boot. He chased me around the garden shouting and kicking out at me. Fortunately for me I was quicker than him. The gate was still open so I ran out into the alley and towards the road, I looked over my shoulder, and the garden gate had been firmly shut.

That was the last time I was to see that garden and the shed. I was on my own and terrified. I skulked off down the road towards the town centre, frightened and confused, where were my mum and my brothers? I headed for the burger bar in the middle of the town where one could normally pick up some nice scraps. I was in luck, for in the top of a full litter bin there were some discarded chips which went down a treat.

I trotted off into a side street near the burger bar and in a dark sheltered alley along side one of the houses, I curled up and went to sleep, but not for long. I awoke with a start and found myself peering into two fierce and frightening green eyes. The cat spat at me as its eyes closed to slits; it lunged at me with outstretched claws but I managed to leap

out of the way. I ran off down the alley and into the road, the cat was close behind me, making a blood curdling scream. With one almighty leap it tried to leap up on to my back, with outstretched claws, but I had seen this so jerked to one side and I was away up the road at full tilt. I hadn't noticed because I dare not look behind, but the cat had given up the chase, it had won! When I did stop and look back I could see the cat in the street lights walking off with a victorious swagger, which I was to learn, only cats, can do so well. I eventually found some thick undergrowth and curled up in its midst. I had had enough excitement for one night.

The next few days were difficult for me. Food was scarce and I began to lose weight. Even around the burger bar there was nothing and I was chased away by the owner on a number of occasions, obviously my presence wasn't wanted. It was during one of the altercations with the burger bar owner, that I was to learn just how hard cars were. I was standing at the door of the premises, enjoying all the delicious scents and licking my lips when the man came running around from behind the counter where I had not seen him. He raced towards me shouting loudly. I ran off and into the road and into the path of a car that was just pulling away from the traffic lights. The front of the car hit me on the head and all went dark.

As I regained consciousness, I could hear voices and became aware that there were a number of people standing over me. My head really hurt and I was having difficulty focussing. I felt someone pick me up and I was carried to a nearby car and placed on the front seat. A lady got into the drivers seat and we drove off. This was a very strange experience and I didn't like it. We travelled a short distance before turning off the road into a car park. The lady got out and at this point I suddenly became fully conscious but my head was pounding.

The lady disappeared into a building and returned shortly after with a man in a white coat. I watched them as they came around to my side of the car and slowly opened the door. The man was holding a short pole with a loop over one end. He tried to slip the loop over my head, but as quick as a flash I leapt out of the seat and between the man's legs and away across the car park. The man chased after me but was no match for me.

I ran out of the car park and dashed across the road narrowly avoiding a car that hooted at me. I ran and ran with a pounding head until I felt I was safe. I panted heavily, my thin sides were heaving with the exertion. I just wanted to rest and I eventually curled up under a big tree behind a house, I was exhausted.

I was awoken some time later by drops of rain falling on me. The drops got heavier and heavier and I sought shelter in a wooden lean to in a garden not far away, it was just in time as the rain became a torrent. I shook myself and sat and looked out through the rain. Suddenly there was a huge flash of white light which startled me. This was followed almost immediately by a loud crash which sent me scuttling into the corner. This was followed by another flash and crash and another. This was my first experience of a thunderstorm and I did not like it at all. The rain continued in torrents for ages. I curled up and tried to sleep but the thunder continued for some time.

# A Friend

I soon learnt that the market square in Saffron Walden was a good place to get scraps and some people were really nice and would give me scraps such as pieces of bread out of their bags. One old lady in particular began to make quite a fuss of me and would bring me titbits every morning. She walked with a walking stick and would always drag a small trolley behind her. I learnt to recognise the sound of the wheels on the footpath as she passed the shops to the square where I would be waiting.

One morning we met up as usual near a large post box and she sat on a nearby bench and she gave me some food which went down a treat. I was really hungry as I hadn't eaten since we met up the previous day. Afterwards I licked her hand as she made a fuss of me. This was something unusual for me and I enjoyed the fuss as much as the food. Eventually she slowly got to her feet and went to walk off. She turned to me and said "Come on then." She didn't have to say that twice, I was by her side in a flash walking past the shops. She kept on talking to me as we cleared the shops. We turned up a small road with houses both sides. I knew this road having rummaged through some dustbins here before.

Eventually we walked through a gate and up a path with grass on both sides of it, to the front door which the lady opened and went in dragging her trolley behind her. I stood nervously at the door until she turned around and said "Come in". I nervously went in and the door was shut behind me. I followed the old lady through to her kitchen where she removed her coat and unpacked a few things out of the trolley and put these away in cupboards, I sat and watched her. She placed a bowl of water on the floor and I drank the lot. She kept on talking to me but I didn't understand what she was saying. We went through to the sitting room where she sat down in a big deep chair and I sat at her feet as she made a big fuss of me. At long last here was someone that was showing me some real kindness and I loved it.

Later she gave me a bowl of bread and milk which was delicious and I was soon licking the empty bowl which was sliding over the kitchen floor. I looked up at the lady, hoping for more but I didn't get any. She opened another door in the kitchen and I went out to explore. The back garden was all grass and had a high wooden fence all around it. There were some interesting scents on the grass including strong cat scents. The lady stood at the door and watched as I investigated every corner before returning back to the house.

As darkness fell much later, the lady placed a thick blanket on the floor in the kitchen and I was shut in there. I soon settled down on the blanket and as I did, I heard the lady's slow footsteps as she went up the stairs. Despite being in strange surroundings I slept very well and didn't wake until I heard the lady's footsteps as she came slowly down the stairs. The kitchen door opened and we greeted each other. I was let out into the garden for my morning toilet after which I raced back in to find a big bowl of bread and milk on the floor which I enjoyed.

Later that morning the lady put her coat on and walked her trolley out of the front door and as she did she said "Are you coming?" I was out of the door like a shot and walking by her side as we walked down the street and back to the shops and the market square. She disappeared into one or two shops while I waited outside standing and guarding her trolley. Every time she returned to the trolley and placed bits into it she would pat me on the head and say "Good girl" With her shopping complete we walked back to her house where I settled down on my bed, while the lady worked in the kitchen. She was talking all the time but I never knew whether she was talking to me or herself!

This routine went on for a few weeks and slowly my skeleton body began to put on some weight but it was a slow process. The lady had started buying tins of meat for me and biscuits. She would give me two meals, one in the morning and one in the evening and I enjoyed them immensely. She had also bought me a leather collar which I did not like very much, it made me scratch my neck all the time until I got used to it. In the evenings I would settle down on the lady's feet as she looked at a curious box which I later learnt was a television. Life was good.

Several weeks later this good life was to change. Early one morning I got up as usual and waited for the lady to come down the stairs and I got ready to greet her as she came through the kitchen door, but she did not appear. I could not understand why she had not come down. By mid morning she still had not appeared and I was getting desperate for the toilet. I began to howl loudly to get her to come down and let me out, but it was in vain. Mid day came and went and she still had not appeared. I continued howling until I heard the front door open and someone came in. The kitchen door opened and in came another lady who I vaguely recognised from the house opposite. She did not speak to me, I don't think she liked me very much. She brushed past me as I tried to greet her and she opened the kitchen door. I ran out into the garden, boy was that a relief!

I came back in and I heard someone come rushing down the stairs and into the kitchen - it was the neighbour again. The back door was closed in a hurry and I was ushered out of the kitchen and along the hall to the front door where I was unceremoniously pushed out, and the front door was slammed shut in my face, with the neighbour inside. I sat on the path, I did not understand what was going on, and where was my friend? A short while later a car pulled up outside and a man got out and walked up the path. He was carrying a small black case. He brushed past me to the front door which opened as he reached it. I tried to follow him in but the door was slammed in my face again. Shortly after another car arrived and a man and a women in uniform got out and walked up the path and passed me. In years to come I was to get used to this uniform. The woman reached down and patted me on the head, as they walked past me. They went into the house and the door was shut again. Shortly after, the first man with the small black case left. I did not understand what was going on.

Quite a while later a large vehicle pulled up outside and two men dressed in black came up the path, wheeling a long trolley with a large long box on top. They disappeared into the house and again I tried to follow but the neighbour told me to "Go away", and the door was shut. I continued to sit outside despite the rain that began to fall, I was confused and miserable, and did not know what to do.

Sometime later, the front door opened and the long trolley with the box on it which was draped in a dark sheet was wheeled out onto the path by the two men and the man and woman in uniform followed it as the trolley was wheeled past me. Despite the heavy rain falling I detected the faint scent of the old lady coming from the drape. The box was placed in the big vehicle and everybody left. A short while later the neighbour came out of the house and closed the door behind her. I went up to her as she hurried down the path but she said in an aggressive tone "Go away dog". I sat at the front door of the house for the rest of the day in the pouring rain, waiting for the old lady to let me in but she did not appear.

I never again saw the old lady that had been so kind to me. The following morning I reluctantly left the house and feeling very miserable and alone, I wandered back down to the market square which was crowded with people. In a litter bin outside one shop I found some stale chips which I ate ravenously until I was chased off by a man. That night as the rain returned with a vengeance I went back to the house of the old lady and curled up at the door all night but the door did not open. The following morning I was back in the market square.

# *Back on the Streets*

I found a good place to sleep at night where I could stay dry. I discovered in a multi storey car park near to a supermarket where people came and went all day, a secluded corner on the ground floor of the car park, behind a huge concrete pillar. I could not be seen and a few dead leaves that had gathered in this corner made the concrete floor more comfortable.

I was checking the bins in the market square one morning but discovered that they had been emptied earlier so I wandered out of the square and up on to the common. Pickings in the bins there were meagre but I picked up an interesting scent coming from a bin near the road that ran along the top of the common. I climbed in and found under some paper a half eaten cheese sandwich. I had got it in my jaws and was in the process of exiting the bin when I heard a loud and angry shout and as I left the bin I saw a man approaching in an aggressive manner. I ran off with the sandwich held firmly in my jaws. I raced across the road between two parked cars. I heard a loud screech of tyres and felt a painful thud on my head and all went black. I don't know how long I was out but when I came to, I felt a lot of pain in my side and blood was pouring from my mouth. As my eyes focused I became aware that there were a lot of people standing around me, including two men in uniform. I was terrified and tried to get to my feet but fell down. The two men in uniform leaned down and tried to pick me up. I felt hands at either end; other people were also trying to help me up. The pain from my side was excruciating, but despite this I got to my feet. Before they could lift me any higher, I came to my senses and ran off between everyone's legs on to the footpath and across the common. Blood was still streaming from my mouth as I ran and I could hear people shouting behind me.

I took a quick glance and saw the two men in uniform chasing after me but I was away and they soon gave up. I cleared the common and had to slow down as the pain from my side hurt. Particularly when I breathed. I could taste the blood in my mouth as I crossed the road by some traffic lights where the cars had stopped. I wandered along the path for quite a while when suddenly a car pulled up sharply next to me and the two men in uniform that had chased me earlier leapt out of the car and approached me. I ran off along the path and shot across the road in front of another car that braked hard and screeched to a halt but I missed him, just!

I ran up a narrow alleyway and out into an area of houses. I had to slow down; the pain was too much from my side. I wandered around for a while trying to find somewhere to rest and eventually curled up under a bush behind a garden fence and went to sleep. My mouth had stopped bleeding but my side was really sore. I slept on and off for two days and stayed where I was. Eventually hunger forced me out from under the bush and I limped off in search of food. It was dark and light rain was falling. In a side road leading off of the market square I found a discarded bag of chips and a half eaten burger on the path, it was still warm. As I devoured the meal I could see a group of youngsters walking away noisily. With a full stomach I went back to my spot in the multi storey car park and slept.

For the next few days I rested a lot in the car park and only came out at night to scavenge for food. It seemed safer at night and there seemed to be more food around, especially chips. Slowly the pain eased in my side and my cut lip and jaw healed over. It was a long time before the pain in my side completely eased, but events were to unfold that caused me pain again.

My life as a stray in Saffron Walden took a number of twists. Some people would feed me and others sent me away with a shout. It was a hard life and I learnt a lot of lessons, but crossing the road was not one of them.

One morning after an unsuccessful night looking for food, I was rummaging through a dustbin in the back garden of a house; there were some interesting morsels in there. I had climbed right in when suddenly I heard the back door of the house open and almost immediately a loud and aggressive shout came from a man standing in the door. I scrambled out of the bin, tipping it over as I leapt out. I ran down the side of the house and through the open gate and narrowly missed two women walking along the path. I shot passed them and out into the road, I heard tyres screeching and felt a hard and very painful thud in my side, then everything went black.

The next thing I remember was the sound of voices above me. My eyes were blurred but I could see shapes of faces looking down at me. I could feel someone trying to pick me up and I felt a number of hands underneath me. I was in a lot of pain from my side again and everything went black as I fell unconscious.

My next recollection was waking up in a large cage at the vet's surgery. I was feeling very groggy and my head was pounding. Everything was spinning around. I tried to stand up but my legs couldn't hold me. I went to move my head when I realised that I had a huge plastic lampshade shaped collar on my neck which came out over my head. My side was really painful and I could feel some sort of patch that was stuck to my side. I felt very weak and tired and I soon went back to sleep.

I don't know how long I had been asleep but I awoke to the sound of the cage door opening and a young girl placed a bowl of food into my cage. I painfully got to my feet and went over to it. I had difficulty eating from the bowl with the collar on but I found that if I pushed hard enough the plastic would bend. The meal was good. I laid back down on the shavings in the cage and licked my lips. I drank some water from another bowl before lying down and going back to sleep, despite the constant yapping from a small mongrel in the opposite cage.

I remained in this cage for a number of days and slowly the pain from my side eased. One morning I was examined by the vet and he prodded my side which hurt a little and I let him know with a gentle whisper. The plastic collar was split and shattered and was taken off. A few days later I was feeling a lot brighter and the pain from my side had turned into a dull ache. A man appeared at the cage door that I recognised as the man that I had run off from before; I believe he was a dog warden.

He was accompanied by two of the girls that had been looking after me, I liked them. The cage door opened and I was helped out of the cage and down on to the ground by the girls. The man then placed a noose around my neck which was attached to a metal pole. I didn't like the noose and tried to pull away but the harder I pulled the tighter it became around my neck and I was gasping for air.

The girls said "Goodbye" to me as I was led out of the door into the car park where I had made my escape before, but there was to be no escape this time. I was lifted unceremoniously into the back of a van and the noose was left around my neck, the pole followed me in, crashing on the metal floor as the doors slammed shut. It was almost dark in the back of the van as I felt it move off. I lay down and awaited my fate.

The journey seemed to go on for ages, until we eventually came to a stop. I could hear voices outside. Suddenly there was a glare of light as the back doors opened and I was momentarily dazzled which was all the time the man needed to grab the pole with the noose attached. I jumped out of the van and immediately noticed that the air was full of the scent of dogs. I could hear a number of dogs barking from within a nearby building which I was led to. I pulled back as hard as I could but the noose tightened around my throat and I had to give way. I was led into the building, a woman who had followed me in went around to the other side of a wooden counter and she and the man spoke for some time. I struggled to get free but it was hopeless. Eventually I was led around the back of the counter and through two sets of doors until I found myself in a long corridor with a concrete floor and cages down each side. There were dogs barking everywhere and the air was pungent with scent. I was dragged down the concrete floor of the corridor, passing cages with some very angry dogs within. There was only a steel mesh separating them from me, I was terrified, I desperately tried to pull away but it was hopeless. One huge German shepherd dog leapt at the steel with such force that the entire cage rattled, I darted forward almost pulling the woman off her feet.

We reached an empty cage at the far end of the corridor, the door was open. I was pushed inside and the noose was removed over my head. I tried to escape but the door was slammed firmly in my face. The woman spoke softly to me and walked off. I looked around at my new 'Home'. At the back of the cage there was a large wooden box with low sides and full of straw. The cage had steel mesh all around with a concrete floor covered in straw. Along the back wall to the side of the box was a large steel plate on tracks fixed to the wall. I could smell fresh air coming from behind the door. I sniffed all around the cage but there was nothing to eat. I sat at the door for ages, staring at the empty cage opposite. The dogs in the other cages began to quieten down. I drank from a bowl of water in the corner of the cage before sitting in the box.

Much later a bowl of food was placed in my cage, I tried to escape but the door was slammed shut. The food was good and I licked the bowl clean. I was very thin, as pickings on the streets in Saffron Walden had been meagre. The bruising on my side could clearly be seen through my thin coat. I curled up in the box sleeping and dreaming of being free back on the streets.

The following morning soon after the lights came on, the steel plate slid open and a sudden blast of fresh air hit me. I was going to escape! I leapt through the door to the outside but found myself in a huge caged in area with a concrete floor; this was my exercise yard. It was a very wet and windy day but despite this I investigated every nook and cranny for an escape route but none were found. I did my toilet and then I heard the inside door open and shut again as I rushed back in. A bowl of food and fresh water had been put in. I emptied the food bowl and licked it clean, washed it down with a good drink before going back outside. I was surprised to meet my neighbour who was also outside in the next pen. She was a small brown young mongrel who was very friendly. We sniffed each other through the wire for some time. From all the scents on her I assumed that she had been here for quite awhile. It began to rain so I eventually went inside and curled up in my box.

The following morning while I was outside, the sliding door slammed shut. I was nervous and stayed close to the little mongrel. A short while later the door opened and I rushed in. The straw had been replaced in the box. I went back outside but my little 'Friend' had gone.

Over the next few days I got used to the routine, there were dogs coming and going all the time, and the noise was incredible. One morning I saw a couple looking at my friend next door through the wire door. They were talking to the woman who fed us. The cage door opened and the little dog ran out and greeted the couple with yaps and tail wagging, this couple were obviously her master and mistress. The man picked her up and she licked his face, everyone was laughing. They walked off, still holding my friend, who looked over his shoulder at me as they disappeared. I curled up in my box and slept, I felt very lonely.

Several days later an event was to happen that was to change my life for ever. It was a warm sunny day and I had spent most of the day outside. A new dog was in next door to me, a Jack Russell terrier who was very friendly. I towered over him as we sniffed each other through the wire. He had a ball to play with and he spent ages throwing the ball and then running and catching it, I couldn't really see the point of that? Suddenly I heard voices inside and the few dogs that were in at the time started barking. I went in to investigate and saw the woman who fed us standing outside my cage with a couple looking down at me. The man was big and had a beard, the woman was smaller. They talked for some time before the cage door was opened and a lead was placed over my head. I was led out, the couple were stroking me, which I liked very much, and I had not had much of this during my short life.

I was led outside and into a large wire pen with grass, this was luxury after what I had been used to. The man then went to a car and a yellow Labrador like me jumped out and was led over to me. She sniffed me through the wire before being allowed in with me. She was about the same age as me but looked a lot healthier. We greeted each other by sniffing each other all over. We ran around the pen; playing with a ball that I had found in the pen. It was great fun. The couple were laughing at us. We played for ages running around, chasing each other and having fun. I let her take the ball most of the time! My bruise began to hurt a little with all this exercise but I didn't care, this was great fun. I soon learnt that her name was 'Chaz'.

As darkness began to fall, Chaz was taken back to the car and I went back to the building on the lead. The man held me on the lead as he and the lady spoke for what seemed like ages to the woman that had fed me. Finally she came around to where I was sitting and patted me on the head and took the lead off and said "Goodbye young one and good luck". The man placed another lead over my head and I was led out of the building and to the car where Chaz was sitting. I jumped in beside her and we sat and looked out of the window as we drove away from the kennels.

A new life was about to begin for me with Chaz, who was to become a close and dear friend. We were to have many adventures together with the couple who I now know as Master and Pat. I had no name when I arrived so they named me 'Chocka' and this is where my story really begins.

Chocka very thin on arrival at new home

Chocka and Chaz on their first night

# *A Home at Last*

My new home was in Thaxted and as soon as I arrived I investigated the house which was called 'Pandemonium' and the garden; there were many interesting scents. My first night I spent with Chaz in the kitchen of the house. We each had our own beds which consisted of large plastic boxes lined with warm soft blankets; this was pure luxury after what I had been used to. Despite this luxurious bed I tried to curl up with Chaz but she was not prepared to share her bed and growled her disapproval. I curled up in my bed and rested my head on my paws and looked at Chaz. I eventually got off to sleep but I had a very disturbed night, I kept on waking up every time there was a sound outside.

Early the following morning Master and Pat came into the kitchen and they greeted us and made a big fuss of us; this was not something I was used to but I could get to like it! We were each given a treat from Master's cereal bowl, Chaz knew what to expect and I soon learnt. This was a routine to last us for the rest of our lives. After our breakfast we both had leads attached and Master and Pat took us for a walk. After a short distance we were out in open fields behind the house. We were released from our leads. This was a real curiosity to me; I had never seen fields before. I was soon running along aside Chaz along a track with Master and Pat way behind. There were no houses or roads and those nasty objects called cars, this was fantastic. I ran at full speed, not after anything in particular just enjoying the freedom, it was beautiful.

Chocka on the left and Chaz on the right

Chaz kept up with me, as she thought I was chasing something, she kept sniffing the ground. I eventually stopped and turned around, Master and Pat were way off in the distance. Chaz and I sat and waited for them, which gave us a chance to get our breath back. Master and Pat arrived and spoke to us, the tone of their voices suggested that they were pleased with us. They patted us and we were given a little treat, I could get used to this. We walked on for ages and when we eventually did get home we both slept in the sun in the garden, this was the life!

As the days went by I got used to the routine at Pandemonium and Chaz even let me share her bed; although she thought she was the lead dog in our relationship, I let her think that, it didn't bother me, we never fought or had a disagreement , I wasn't interested in all that malarkey. There was a constant stream of visitors to the house. We were always greeted and had a fuss made of us which we both loved.

One visitor in particular who became a good friend to us was a little man called 'Mac' who lived a few doors away and was obviously a close friend of Master and Pat... We liked him a lot as he would always bring us treats in his pockets, tiny biscuits. He would hand us the treats quietly so Master and Pat didn't see. He would often come for dinner and would quietly slip us something off the table. He would sometimes come in for the day to look after us if Master and Pat were out. We loved that because he would spoil us all day and we would sleep at his feet waiting for the next treat.

# *The Sea*

Early one morning Master gave us a very brisk walk in the semi dark and as soon as we were back we were bundled into the car, as usual Chaz had to be lifted in. I could never understand why she couldn't jump in like me, she always needed help in. We were soon off and Chaz and I settled down and went to sleep. It was a long journey but eventually the car stopped and we were let out on our leads. There was a curious building next to the car park which I later learnt was Cromer Lighthouse. There was a strong cold breeze blowing and a curious scent on the wind. We began to climb down a long line of wooden steps and as we did the strange scent grew stronger. Down and down we went. We passed a man with a terrier on a lead walking up. I wanted to go and say 'hello' but I was held firmly by Pat.

Eventually we reached the bottom and stepped out on a strange soft surface that squeezed up between my toes, it was sand and I had never seen this before. We were let off our leads and we both ran off excitedly towards a huge mass of water with waves breaking onto the sand. This was where the curious scent was coming from. Chaz ran straight in, I was a little more cautious, but eventually we were both swimming and riding in on the waves, which was great fun. My only problem was that I was swallowing a lot of water in my excitement. Master and Pat were walking along the sand at the water's edge, they were laughing at our antics. One particularly large wave came in and picked us up and dumped us unceremoniously on the sand. We shook ourselves and ran back in again, this really was great fun. Another big wave took me off my feet and carried me back on to the sand, Chaz landed near me. I had had enough so after a good shake I ran over to Master and Pat, while Chaz went back in.

Master had a ball which he threw and which I chased after, caught and brought back. He threw it again and I caught it again. Chaz was barking excitedly as the waves were getting bigger so I dropped the ball at Pat's feet and ran back into the sea, only to be knocked back by a huge wave, I swallowed another mouthful of salty water, and coughed and spluttered. Master called me over to him and I shook myself close to him, he was not amused. Chaz eventually joined us and we walked along the sand. Pat threw the ball and we chased after it, sometimes I would catch it and other times I left it for Chaz.

Eventually we climbed back up the long line of steps to the car park. Pat dried us off as best as she could with towels before we were allowed back into the car, Chaz needed her usual help up. We settled down, we were both exhausted. Master and Pat disappeared for a long time, it was dark when they returned, and a single light in the car park was shining into the car. We drove out of the car park and began our long journey home. I wasn't feeling too well, I think I had swallowed too much sea water and we were both sick on the way home; although Pat and Master didn't discover this until we jumped out back at home. We were soon snugly back in our beds and sound asleep. I dreamt of giant waves all night.

# A Deer

As the year moved on the countryside around our home changed. The fields were harvested leaving stubble which was difficult and uncomfortable to walk or run on. This in turn changed to fresh soil which when wet was very sticky and difficult to run on. Chaz and I would investigate all the scents left by the previous night. There were scent trails everywhere and it was great fun investigating them.

One morning we were across the fields with Pat. It was sunny but there was a strong cold breeze blowing, which carried the scents in the air. Chaz and I were on a track walking alongside Pat when we both picked up a strong and interesting scent which appeared to be coming from a hedge to the side of us; we went to investigate. We crashed through the hedge and there in the middle of the field were two tall animals standing still. On seeing us they immediately began running away. Chaz gave out her customary excited bark and began running, I ran along side her. I didn't know what these animals were but boy could they shift. Pat was calling us but these creatures were much more interesting.

They disappeared through a hedge way ahead of us and by the time we had gone through the hedge they were no where to be seen, but their scent was strong on the ground so we followed the trail. This eventually led us to a large wood on the other side of the field and we were soon passing the tall trees all around us. The scent was not so easy to follow in the wood but on we went.

We were both panting heavily and Pat's voice had all but disappeared. We had lost the scent so we followed our own scent back and eventually saw Pat on the path, not far from where we had left her. She greeted us as she put our leads on.

We both slept very well that night and Chaz snored!

# *The strange time of the year*

As the daylight hours grew shorter and the air grew colder it came to the strange time of the year when curious lights were put up all around Thaxted. A huge tree appeared outside the Guildhall with strange lights all over it. I had seen it during my early days in Saffron Walden.

It was not just outside but in our house as well. A tree was brought in and stood in one corner. Pat covered it in lights and lots of other glittering bits and chocolates in strange wrappers. Chaz and I sat and watched until she had finished and then we both went over and sniffed out the chocolates. We were then told very sternly "No" by Pat, we got the message, although Chaz did try and steal one on one occasion, but she got caught!

For several days people called in, many of whom we recognised. One particular day a large number of people arrived, including Mac, Ian, Beccy, Phil and others. They all eventually sat around a large table and began eating. The air was full of mouth watering scents. Chaz and I sat under the table near Mac's feet, we knew that he would treat us with some little morsels; we were not disappointed, the turkey tasted delicious!

We were given little treats all through the day. I later learnt that this time of the year was known as 'Christmas'. I decided that I for one really do like Christmas!

Soon after, the tree was removed and everything packed away. Christmas was soon a distant memory as we were preoccupied with snow for a few days - playing in the snow across the fields on our walks with Pat and Master during the day and curling up in front of the fire in the evening.

# *Deep Snow!*

Soon after that first fall of snow had gone the weather turned really cold, Chaz and I spent most of our time in front of the fire. After one particularly cold windy night, the morning revealed a deep covering of snow in the garden. Chaz and I had a good play in the snow. After breakfast our collars and leads were put on and Pat, Master and Mac took us for a walk. Everything was a dazzling white in the sunlight. We went out into the fields behind the house where we were let off our leads. The snow was really deep, almost up to my chest, I heard Master call them "Drifts"

I jumped into a particularly deep one and sank deep down. I was immediately followed by Chaz. The snow caved in on us but we managed to pull ourselves out. Master and Pat were laughing at us. We were both covered in snow until we shook ourselves next to Mac who was laughing. The snow had covered any scent and the air was crisp, clear and very cold.

We walked on up towards the woods with Master and Pat throwing balls of snow at us. Chaz was catching them in her mouth. I jumped up to catch one that Mac had thrown at me and I fell back into a deep drift in a ditch. Chaz thought this was great fun and leapt in on top of me again which pushed me even deeper into the snow. She clambered out but I was having some difficulty until a hand grabbed me by the scruff of my neck and lifted me out. The hand belonged to Master who was on his knees laughing. I shook myself next to him, showering him in snow, everybody laughed.

We eventually reached the wood and as I went in, a particularly large piece of snow fell off one of the tall trees and struck me on the nose which startled me. I ran back to Master who was laughing. Pat and Mac had gone on ahead with Chaz. I decided not to go into the wood! I soon caught Chaz up as we passed the wood and were back out into the white barren landscape where the fields had once been and now was snow as far as the eye could see. Suddenly Chaz was onto a scent of something and I followed her into a hedge just as a pheasant exploded out of the hedge and flew over our heads, showering us in snow. I watched as it flew into the clear blue sky and away.

A little further on another pheasant took flight and swore at us as we tried to chase it through the deep snow;

we soon gave up. It disappeared over the wood still calling. We didn't go much further on before Pat and the others turned around and began walking back. We followed in their footprints, it made for easier going. We eventually got back to the house where we were dried off with towels before curling up in front of the fire while Mac, Pat and Master sat around talking.

The snow lasted a few days and was great fun. It disappeared as quickly as it had arrived leaving a lot of water around, it was very muddy across the fields!

# *My First Operation*

Chaz and I were bundled into the car early one morning by Pat. Master had left early in his uniform. We drove off from Thaxted but were only in the car for a short time before we were leaping out on our leads. The air was full of scents and Chaz and I investigated many scents on the grass on the edge of the car park before we were led into the building.

We walked into a room where there were a number of people sitting around. The air was full of some very interesting scents, but Pat kept us on very short leads. A women sitting next to us was holding on tight to a brown and white terrier that looked very friendly so I drew close to it to say "Hello" but I was greeted by a sudden snap and the baring of teeth as a warning. Pat pulled me back and held me tight, all I wanted to do was say "Hello".

Eventually we were led through to another room where a man, the vet was standing by a tall table. Chaz was told to sit and she did, while I was lifted on to a table. The vet then prodded and poked me all over and spoke to Pat. A few minutes later Pat and Chaz left the room, a young girl came in and led me through to another big room where there were a number of large cages; I was placed in one, I did not want to go in but the girl gently pushed me in and closed the door. I didn't like it in there at all. I stood at the cage door and watched as the girl left.

I paced around the cage for a while before laying down. I had had no breakfast that morning and was beginning to feel quite hungry. Much later another girl came in and I was led out of the cage and out of that room and into another where the vet was standing with another girl. There was a curious scent in that room. I was lifted up on to a table and as I looked around to see if I could escape I felt a sharp jab in the back of my neck and almost immediately the room began spinning and then went black.

When I awoke I was back in the cage and as I came to I realised that I had a huge 'lampshade' collar attached to my neck. My tummy was very sore and I was very groggy and I soon went back to sleep. I was awoken some time later by the sound of the door to the room opening and a girl walked in and she was leading a huge dog in. He was a handsome beast albeit a mixture of a number of breeds. He was placed in a cage opposite me. We sat and looked at each other for some time; I must have looked strange with the lampshade on. My tummy was still sore so I laid down which seemed to help.

A short while later the dog opposite was led out of the room and I did not see him again, for shortly after the room door opened and a girl came in with Pat behind her. Boy was I pleased to see her! I was let out of the cage and I banged the collar on the side of the cage as I came out in my excitement to greet Pat, which in itself was not easy with this collar on. I tried to jump up and greet her but I got a severe pain from my tummy.

I was led out of the building and Pat gently lifted me into the back of the car. I laid down for the short journey home. I was helped out of the car and into the house where I was greeted by my pal Chaz, the hood made it difficult to lick each other but we managed. Later in the evening I was given a small bowl of food but although it was lovely it did not stay down long.

I did not sleep very well that night, with the pain from my tummy and the hood; I slept off and on for most of the following day but I did manage to keep my breakfast down. Chaz and Master went for a walk but I was not interested. As the days went by the soreness from my tummy disappeared but I was having problems with the collar. I kept on banging into things. But the worst thing was that I couldn't scratch my neck, ears or my face which was really frustrating.

Chaz accompanied me when we went back to the vets a few days later. The stitches were removed from my tummy which was quite a relief as they were beginning to itch. The 'lampshade' or should I say what was left of it was removed. It had taken quite a bashing. My operation scar soon healed and Chaz and I were back across the fields again together, running and chasing each other as if nothing had happened.

Chocka with hood

# *On Holiday*

As the months went by I began to put on some weight and felt a lot fitter. I was painfully thin when I had arrived at Pandemonium. Early one morning we went for a walk as usual across the fields, Master was walking quite briskly and Chaz and I had a good run in the warm sunshine. When we got back there were 2 large suitcases and our beds on the path by Master's Land rover. They were put in the back and we followed. I leapt into the back but Chaz could not and Master had to help her. We sat and watched out of the windows as the last bits were put in and we were off. We sat and watched excitedly but after a while we settled down and slept. I dreamt of the fields behind the house.

We had a long journey before turning off into a gateway into a big house with a huge tree to one side. Chaz was becoming very excited; obviously she had been before and recognised the scents. We were let out as we were met by a man that Chaz obviously knew. He greeted us both as he led us into his huge garden. I later learnt from the conversations that his name was Peter and he was Pat's

Sheep in Bracken

father. We ran around the garden, there was the strong smell of rabbit and squirrel everywhere. Master and Pat unloaded the land rover, including our beds that were placed on the kitchen floor and our water bowls which were filled, I emptied one bowl; I was thirsty.

Eventually Pat called us in and our collars and leads were put on. This usually meant a walk and we both got very excited. As we left the house Master said "Calm down you two" as we pulled hard on the leads. Pat and Peter followed on behind, talking. We walked off down a tree lined lane on a steep hill and at the bottom we turned off through a gate into an area covered in bracken with the odd small tree here and there. The sun was shining and there was a gentle breeze. Chaz and I were very excited, we wanted to go off and investigate some interesting scents. Suddenly, I was startled when I saw a sheep in amongst the bracken. I barked and ran back on my lead to Master's side. I hadn't seen one of these curious creatures before. As we approached it on the track it moved off, I was not at all certain about it. Master would not let us off our leads and in fact he shortened them so we were close into his side.

We walked on and on until we reached another gate with a curious metal grid in the ground across the entrance. After passing through the gate Master released us from our leads and we ran off. I didn't know which way to go first. There were so many scents, there were no sheep in this part of the forest which I had heard Pat refer to as Ashdown Forest. I followed Chaz and she eventually found a log to carry, she was happy. It was thrown for her on a number of occasions and she retrieved it from the bracken. We came upon a large pool of water and both of us ran in, despite

Chocka ahead of Chaz

Master shouting "No", we didn't hear him! The water was quite deep and cool and a little muddy. We both laid down and the water was up to our shoulders, it was lovely. Master called us out and eventually we gave in and came out and trotted over to him, where we shook all the water and mud off, from the tone of Master's voice he was not happy! Peter and Pat were laughing behind him. I couldn't see what all the fuss was for; we had come out of the water as requested.

We ran off through the bracken, Chaz had found another log to carry. We walked on for ages before we came off the forest and found ourselves back at the house. Our coats were dry, but Pat gave us a brush down which I thoroughly enjoyed. Our beds were in the kitchen and we soon settled down and slept. I dreamt of the sheep in the forest, they were chasing me!

The following morning after our breakfast and a quick run around the garden, our leads were on and we were off with Master back up to the forest. We passed through where the sheep were and after crossing the iron grill Chaz and I were running free again. We had a quick dip in the pond but Master was walking quite fast and we were soon chasing after him. With some other dogs approaching in the distance our leads were put back on, we left the main track and walked quickly down a narrow track with bracken on both sides. The sun was hot and our coats were drying quickly.

On and on we walked, Master was keeping up a good pace. Suddenly I spotted something coiled up in the middle of the path in the sun. I ran forward and Chaz followed. Suddenly I heard Master shout "No" and I felt a violent jerk on my lead which almost took me off my feet. Chaz had been pulled up as well. Master rushed up to us and held us firm only feet from the coil, he obviously did not want us to approach it. We stood and watched as the coil suddenly unravelled and the snake slid away into the bracken. Master turned us around and led us back to the main track. He told us that the snake was in fact an "Adder" and that it was "Poisonous" whatever that meant?

The walks up on to the forest became our regular routine with a walk in the morning and in the afternoon. We never saw another snake but there were many scents to investigate everyday. One morning we were up on the forest with Master, Pat and Peter. We had passed over the metal grid and were off the leads. Chaz had picked up a strong scent of a fox deep in the bracken and became very excited barking as she ran, crashing through the dense undergrowth. I followed close behind her. We ran around in a huge arc and eventually found ourselves back on the track, way ahead of Master and the others. They were all calling us. We followed the scent back into the bracken on the other side of the track but then we became totally confused as the scent crisscrossed all over the place, the fox had completely confused us. Try as we could we could not find the trail again, the fox's scent was everywhere. We were both panting heavily as the dense bracken had taken it's toll on us. We heard Master and the others approaching so we returned to the track whereupon our leads were fastened back on. I dreamt of foxes that night and I think Chaz did as well. She woke me up on one occasion whimpering loudly in her sleep and her legs and feet were giving the impression that she was running as she laid on her bed.

Our holiday at the Ashdown forest came to an abrupt end one morning. We had had our customary walk on the forest with Pat. When we returned to the house Master was loading cases and our beds into the car. Eventually we were beckoned to the back, I leapt in but Chaz had to be helped in as usual. As we drove out of the drive Chaz and I were looking out of the back window and we saw Peter waving. We soon settled down and slept, I went into a really deep sleep. When I awoke we were in the drive back at our home in Thaxted. We ran through to the back garden where there was a strong scent of cat. Chaz became very excited and went exploring all around the garden until Pat shouted at Chaz who was walking through the flower beds, something I learnt very quickly was a big no, no.

A few days after we had returned home, we were to have another incident involving a fox. We were across the fields behind the house, Master had let us off the leads and he and Pat were in deep conversation. I suddenly picked up a strong scent of fox in a dry ditch on the edge of a wood. The scent led into the wood and I went to investigate, Chaz followed; it was not long before the scent grew stronger and stronger and we were both running flat out. Chaz was barking excitedly, I could never really understand why she did that. I could hear Master and Pat calling way off in the distance but chose to ignore them; the fox was a lot more fun. The trail led us out of the wood and into a huge field of stubble. I immediately spotted our quarry way off in the distance. I accelerated away and left Chaz behind me.

The fox was very quick and soon disappeared through a hedge, I was still some way from it and Chaz was far behind me but still barking excitedly. I eventually passed through the hole in the hedge where the fox had gone, there was no sign of it on the other side. The scent trail was very confusing; it appeared to go around in a large circle and crossed over itself several times. Chaz had caught me up and we both cast around trying to pick up the trail but it was hopeless, the fox had made good it's escape. We eventually lost interest and followed our trail back to the wood and the path beyond, where we met up with Master and Pat. We were put back on our leads for the remainder of the walk. We were to have many more interesting encounters with foxes in the years to come. I slept well that night.

# The Downs

Very early one morning Master gave us a very short walk before bundling us into the car. Our empty water bowls and leads were also placed alongside us. We were soon leaving Thaxted. Chaz and I were sitting up watching for quite awhile before laying down and going to sleep. We travelled for a long time before turning off the road and travelled along a track, which eventually lead to a small car park where we stopped. Chaz and I were sitting and looking out of the windows excitedly, there were some very interesting scents coming into the car. Master turned around to us and said "Well you two this is the South Downs". I had no idea what he meant, but it certainly looked a nice place to explore.

The rear door was opened slowly and we tried to jump out but we were held back until our leads were put on. Then we were out and investigating some strange scents that were in an unusual soil which was white and which stuck to our paws. We both got very impatient as Master and Pat put on different shoes. Our water bowl was filled from a bottle but neither of us were really interested, there was too much going on.

Eventually we walked off and passed through two sets of gates before beginning to climb a hill that I had heard Master refer to as 'Cissbury Ring' The grass was short and stubbly as we strained on the leads to investigate everything. We eventually found ourselves on a white track which we climbed for quite awhile, eventually reaching the very top of the hill, where we were finally let off our leads, freedom! There was rabbit scent everywhere and we ran around investigating many holes but we saw no rabbits. The sun was high in the sky and there was a strong breeze blowing.

Master and Pat sat down on the grass while we went off and investigated further afield but always keeping the two in sight. On the other side of the hill we met another dog that appeared from behind a bush. He was smaller than us and of mixed breed. We greeted each other and played for a short time before his master placed him back onto his lead and left. We learnt that his name was 'Oscar' and he was very friendly and we saw him again when we returned to Master and Pat who were sitting and eating. 'Oscar' and his master passed along a track just below us. We trotted down to see him again and he was let off his lead. We had a good run around and a game of 'Chase' while his master spoke to Pat and Master for quite awhile, they were all laughing at our antics. Eventually Oscar was called back in and placed back on his lead, and they left.

We sat down on the grass next to our two, who finished their picnic. There were a couple of birds singing high in the sky above us and I looked up at them with some curiosity. Master said that they were "Skylarks" what ever that meant; all I knew was that they were very loud. We were given a couple of treats before our leads were put back on and we walked off. We walked right around the top of the hill and passed a concrete plinth that had numerous scents of dogs all around it. Pat said that it was a "Trig Point" I had not got a clue what that was?

Half way down the hill on the other side we passed through a gate and a big metal grid in the ground in front of the gate. We were still on a fairly steep slope on the hill and there were some curious woolly white creatures moving around on the slope. They appeared to be eating grass! Both Chaz and I were interested in going over to them to investigate them but we were held very firm by our handlers! I later learnt from Pat that these were sheep and we were never to go near them, I think we both got the message.

Back at the car much later we were offered the bowl of water again and this time we emptied it between us. We were back in the car and we left the car park. We both settled down to sleep, we were both exhausted, but our rest did not last long before we stopped outside this house. Master and Pat got out and Master said "You two stay there we won't be long" and the door was shut. I don't know how we were supposed to get out! There was plenty of fresh air coming in and we could smell the sea again. We settled down and slept.

Much later Master and Pat returned with two other women who got into the car. Chaz and I greeted them over the seat. Their scents were similar to Master's and I later learnt from Master that these two were his mother and sister, Corinne, and we were in Worthing. We drove for a while before turning off again and driving along a short track which led to a tree shaded car park. Our leads were put back on and we all went for a walk along another white tree-lined track which eventually opened out onto another grass covered hill. We were let off our leads again and we were off investigating, there were no sheep unfortunately. We kept the others in sight as they walked along a path towards a large clump of tall trees, which I later learnt was 'Chanctonbury Ring'

On reaching the trees they all sat down on a fallen tree and talked for some time. There were those birds singing above our heads as we ran around. We had a game of chase through the trees for quite a while before collapsing in heaps at Master and Pat's feet. We sat there for quite a while before we all went for a walk around the trees and the hill. The sun was setting when we returned to the car and returned to the house where we had collected Corinne and Master's mum. We slept in the car while Master and Pat were in the house and it was quite a while before they returned to the car and we set off for home in the dark. We slept all the way home.

Back on our beds I dreamt of the downs and those curious creatures called 'Sheep'.

# *Trees, Trees and more Trees*

Mac arrived early one morning and gave us both a little treat while Master and Pat were not looking. We were placed into the car, Chaz needed helping as usual. Mac got in and Pat was in the back and Master was driving. We both looked out of the back window as we left Thaxted and drove through open countryside. We eventually laid down and listened to Mac and the others talking. We were not driving for long before we turned into a large car park. There were some interesting scents coming into the car which made Chaz and I sit up excitedly. Our leads were attached to our collars before we were allowed to jump out of the car. There were no other cars in the car park but the ground had many interesting scents. We all walked off to a gate which we passed through and we soon found ourselves deep within an area of tall trees.

Mac, Pat and Master were busy talking but our leads were held firm. Chaz and I wanted to go off and investigate but we couldn't. On and on we went and it got darker and darker. From the conversations that the others were having I learnt that this place was called 'Hatfield Forest' and by all accounts it appeared to be very special. There were huge trees everywhere and the ground was cold and damp, the sunlight could not penetrate the leaf canopy above our heads. I had detected fresh fox, rabbit and deer scent on the ground and a scent that I was not sure of, but we could not go off for some reason.

On and on we walked through the trees until we eventually came out into sunlight and there was a huge expanse of water ahead of us. There were lots of interesting birds on the water and flying over it, but still we were held back. We walked along a path that ran beside the lake which had trees all around it. We eventually passed through another gate and we were then let off our leads. The trees here were huge and close together and it was very dark once we moved back into the forest. Chaz and I went off to investigate and I soon discovered who owned the scent that I did not recognise earlier. I suddenly saw ahead of me a small grey creature with a bushy tail. I chased after it but it ran up the trunk of a nearby tree and was gone. I then saw another one at the same time as Chaz saw it, we both chased it but it also scampered up a tree, how did they do that? We saw several more as we walked deeper and deeper into the trees. Pat later told us that they were "Grey Squirrels"; all I knew was that they could move incredibly fast and boy could they climb trees, but they were good fun to chase even if we had no chance of catching them.

Eventually we saw daylight ahead and Master called us in and our leads were re-attached. We were quite exhausted when we got back into the car and returned home. I dreamt of giant squirrels for the rest of the day.

# The Move

During the late summer at the house events began to occur which were to eventually change my life for ever. One evening Master had come home in uniform as usual but on this occasion he appeared to be very excited. He quickly changed, him and Pat left in the car. We were in the kitchen a little confused. They returned sometime later and were talking about a "Cottage" whatever that meant I did not know but soon all was to be revealed. As the warm summer progressed the air of excitement continued with my owners.

One morning after our usual walk with Pat we came back to find that Master had a trailer hitched up to his Land rover and it was full of bits from the sheds. Chaz and I were bundled into the back of Pats car, Chaz needed help as usual. We went for a short drive before turning into a farm yard where we drove through and out into a field behind. On the other side we stopped behind a cottage behind a tall hedge. We were let out and we investigated the field for scents, while Master and Pat unloaded the trailer in the corner of the field immediately behind the cottage. Little did Chaz and I realise how significant this action was going to be. We returned to Thaxted where another load was placed in the trailer and we would return to the field where it was all unloaded and covered with a sheet.

The following day chaos reigned as Pat, Master and 4 other men spent the whole day packing stuff into boxes; Chaz and I kept out of the way as we didn't want to get packed into a box! It was obvious to us that something major was happening. By the end of the day everything was packed, except our beds, which we were guarding and our water bowls. The house looked completely bare and Chaz and I slept very uneasily that night.

The following morning at the crack of dawn, two huge Lorries arrived at the front of the house and the 4 men that were here yesterday arrived along with 3 others. They began carrying all the boxes and furniture out and into the Lorries. Chaz and I watched on from the comfort of our beds. Eventually Master called us outside and we got into the car, Chaz needed a lift up! Our beds were loaded around us and other bits and pieces came in as well before we set off. I looked out of the rear window and could see the Lorries outside of the house. This was the last time we were to see the house. A few minutes later we were turning into the driveway of the cottage.

Chaz got really excited and when the back door was opened she jumped out unaided, a first for her, I followed. We ran around investigating the garden which was huge. The field at the back was fenced and levelled and grass was coming through. The tall hedge that separated the cottage from the field had gone, only a bank of dirt remained. A

pond had been dug and the fish from our old home were swimming around in there. There were some interesting scents in the garden, especially at the bottom end where there was strong scent of fox. While we were still investigating the garden the first of the two Lorries arrived and the contents were unloaded into the cottage. We watched as our beds were unloaded from the car and placed in a small back room near the back door. The first lorry left and the second was soon reversing into the front yard and furniture began to emerge. As the sun began to set the second lorry left and Chaz and I began to investigate inside. There was not a lot to see except boxes towering over us. However there was a narrow corridor between the box columns which allowed us to move from one room to another.

Later that evening we found Master and Pat sitting on a settee surrounded by columns of boxes with a bottle on a small table and two full glasses which they chinked together and Master said "Here's to the new "Pandemonium" and they looked at us and smiled. I didn't know what it meant, but I felt that it was good. Chaz and I settled down in our beds and despite the new surroundings, sounds and scents, we both slept well after all the excitement of that day, which was to change our lives again.

The following morning we were let out into the garden early, the fox had been in over- night at the bottom end, Chaz got really excited. Later we went with Pat and Master for our first walk around the farm. We both strained on our leads as there was so much we wanted to investigate.

We walked along the river to a huge expanse of water, Master told us that it was a "Reservoir" all I know is that Chaz was in like a shot swimming around, I was a little more reluctant, but I had a paddle in the shallows. We walked through a large orchard and there was the scent of rabbit and fox everywhere. The farm was to become our territory and we walked it every day. We were to have many adventures over the years.

Soon after we arrived back at the cottage, we met Peter and Jan and their dog 'Pippa' another female yellow Labrador. We were to become good friends over the years, and like Mac, Peter would spoil us with little treats every time we saw him; he always had something in his pocket.

Over the next few days the columns of boxes throughout the cottage rapidly reduced, as Master and Pat emptied and cleared them. Pat was doing most of the clearing as Master would disappear in uniform early in the morning only to return much later in the day. For our part

Chaz and I would patrol our garden as the new grass grew longer.

As Christmas approached Master and Pat spent some time in the garden, planting a lot of trees all the way down one side of the garden and began digging down the other side.

Our first Christmas at the cottage was chaotic as usual. The fire kept us warm, it was pretty cold outside. Mac joined us for a few days and spoilt us something rotten. Master and Pats sons, daughters and partners Beccy, Ian, Phil, Sarah, Gina and Stuart all spent time with us. There was a constant and beautiful smell of cooking coming from the kitchen, and we often had tasty gravy mixed in with our breakfast with the leftovers from the night before.

Life quietened down a little after Christmas but the garden took on a new appearance with the arrival of deep snow. The reservoir froze over and Chaz was unable to swim. We had great fun running and rolling in the snow and catching balls of snow that Master and Pat would throw at us; the snow would explode in our faces. With the extreme cold outside it was nice to curl up in front of the fire in the evening, and when I got too hot I would go and sleep on either Pat's or Master's feet.

The snow didn't last long and spring arrived early and birds began nesting around the farm.

# *The Big Swim*

The large pond in the garden was a definite 'No No' as far as we were concerned and this we learnt early on at the cottage, however the reservoir was alright. For several weeks we had not visited the reservoir, despite it being at the end of the garden. We had been taken to other parts of the farm.

One morning however we were out with Master and we were both off our leads. Master was approaching the steps that lead to the reservoir; we both sat at the bottom and looked at him as he approached. He looked at us and said "Go on then" and we were up the steps in a flash. As Master reached the top of the steps, Chaz already had a big stick and dropped it in front of him. He picked it up and threw it out a long way across the water. Chaz took a huge leap off the top of the bank and crashed into the water and began swimming towards the floating stick. She reached it after a good swim and brought it back to Master. She shook herself right next to him, he was not too pleased.

We walked on around the water which was glistening in the sunlight. Master threw the stick into the water again and Chaz leapt off the bank but she hit the water with an almighty splash. At that point a duck swam out of a nearby reed bed, quacking and scolding at Chaz. She was followed by 4 feathered ducklings which were nearly as big as her. Chaz forgot all about the stick and began to follow them. I was in the shallows and the excitement was too much for me so I began swimming after Chaz and the ducks ahead of her, this was good fun. Master stood watching from the bank. On and on we swam, but we were not gaining on the ducks, who did not appear to be too concerned with us behind them, but they did have a secret weapon! The water was cool and quite choppy with the strong breeze that had got up. We were swimming down the reservoir from one end to the other. I kept my eye firmly on the ducks despite the waves continually splashing my face. Chaz was beginning to tire and I had drawn up alongside her, the ducks were a long way ahead of us by now.

On and on we went and I drew ahead of Chaz but we were still not gaining on the ducks. We were approaching the far end bank of the reservoir when suddenly and without warning all the ducks took off noisily, banked around and flew over our heads. I watched as they disappeared from view. I swam to the bank and climbed out, Chaz soon followed. Master was standing at the top smiling; I think he knew what the ducks were going to do, flight was their secret weapon. We shook ourselves and Master placed us back on our leads for the walk home.

I slept well that night and you can guess what I dreamt of?

# *A Naughty Adventure*

One morning after breakfast and our cereal treats from Masters bowl. Master placed our collars on. Chaz as usual played him up by not sitting down when he told her to, she would try it on every morning with him but he always won. I don't know to this day why she did it.

We walked out across the fields towards the orchard; the ground was full of scent. There was a strong sweet scent coming from the orchard, the trees were covered in blossom. Master let us off our leads in the orchard and we ran around checking the ground for any recent scents. Chaz found it, a strong scent of a deer that had quite recently passed through the trees. We began to follow it excitedly. Master called to us but the scent was a lot more interesting. We ran through the hedge and across a small field to another thick hedge. We found a gap that the deer had used and went through it into a huge field the other side.

Chaz and I were running side by side across the field towards a large wood in the distance. We could still hear the faint voice of Master calling. We eventually reached the wood and disappeared within. We still had not seen any deer we were simply following their scent. It was dark and dense in the wood and we were forced to slow down. The scent was growing stronger, as we left the wood on the other side and came out into a field. As we did we both spotted 4 deer on the other side of the field! Chaz gave out an excited yelp as we ran flat out across the now empty field; the deer had departed with a huge turn of speed.

We ran across the field and through the hedge where the deer had run through and we found ourselves in another huge field. Chaz soon found the scent and we were running straight through the middle of this field. We were beginning to tire a little but on we went. We eventually reached the other side and went through an open gateway and found ourselves on a road. We had lost the scent. We didn't know where we were but we saw a large entrance into some buildings and there were men and women walking around in uniform, not the same as Master's. We walked up a driveway to a barrier where two men were standing. They looked at us and smiled, we must have looked quite a sight, we were covered in mud and panting heavily. They spoke to us and we were led to a nearby room where there were a number of people. They made a fuss of us and we were given a bowl of water, and some biscuits, I liked these people!

A short while later a face appeared in the room that we recognised. It was Master and he did not look very happy and the tone of his voice said it all. He spoke briefly to one man who appeared to be in charge, the others were calling him "Sir" and we were led out and into Master's car, Chaz was helped in rather unceremoniously. Before we left Master turned around to us and said "What do you think you were doing you bad dogs" - the tone said it all!

Back at the cottage Pat hosed us down and cleaned us up and then rubbed us down with a towel. She hardly spoke to us the entire time. We slept for the rest of the day as our coats slowly dried out; we still had our thick winter coats. I dreamt of chasing giant deer. The following morning Master left the house early in his uniform, we did not see him for the rest of the day. Pat took us for a short walk on our leads, we were both very stiff, I can't think why? That night Master sat in his usual chair and we both went up to him and licked his hands and he made a fuss of us, we were forgiven. We slept deeply on his feet.

# *A lovely Scent*

Being back in favour with Master was to be short lived for me, when I found something excellent to roll in one morning. Master had taken us up to the reservoir and Chaz was swimming as usual. As we walked around I found an interesting scent to investigate. Master was busy throwing a stick in for Chaz and was not watching me.

I found a huge dead rotting fish on the bank, it was covered in flies. I decided to roll in it. All around my neck and all down my back and legs, I was in ecstasy and continued rolling until I heard Master shout at me as he came over to see what I had found. I got one more massive roll in before he arrived. I moved away, smelling beautiful. Master looked at the fish and then at me and said "You disgusting dog" the tone suggested that he was not best pleased with me. I went over to him but I was greeted with "Go away you disgusting dog you stink"

On the way home I was kept at arms length and I was given a thorough hose down and shampoo when we got back. I could not understand what all the fuss was about.

Well I thought it was lovely anyway.

# *Good food and a lovely bed*

At a certain time of the year on the farm we discovered that there was a lot of lovely food to eat as the fruit in the orchard ripened and a lot dropped onto the ground. There were apples, and plums in their hundreds and we had a feast. The fruit was really sweet and delicious and we both had our fill, we really did like this time of the year!

It was during one these times that Chaz and I became aware that there was an air of expectation in the cottage with a lot of excitement from Master and Pat. One morning Master carried down the stairs a large suitcase which was placed in one of the cars. We knew that something was happening. Pat got in the car and Master opened the gate and waved as the car left. Master closed the gate and said to us "It's alright dogs she will be back soon"

Master took us for a walk and we had our fill of apples, the plums were all but finished. The rest of the day we spent on the lawn in the sun, moving out of the way of the tractor that Master was driving to cut the grass.

That evening, Master lit the fire and we settled down on his feet for the evening, it was nice and warm; I went into a deep sleep and dreamt of giant plums. Much later Master turned the lights out and we knew it was bed time, but instead of being settled down in our beds with a little treat, Master went up the stairs and left the gate open at the bottom of the stairs. We both stood and watched as he reached the top stair. He turned and looked at us and said "Come on then". Chaz needed no other encouragement, she was up those stairs like a shot, I followed cautiously, I knew we were not usually allowed up stairs, which is why there was a gate at the bottom.

After finishing in the bathroom we followed him into the bedroom. Eventually he got into bed and all but disappeared under the covers; we both sat and looked at him inquisitively. He looked down at us and said "Come on up then", within seconds we were up on the bed licking his face. He was laughing out loud and was saying "Stop it and settle down". We eventually curled up on the covers and before long we were both in a deep sleep. During the night some strange noises came from Master, he was snoring!

We woke Master up early by licking his face, he laughed as he got up. After breakfast we were out across the fields again and into the orchard. It was raining heavily but the fruit still tasted lovely. There was no sign of Pat despite Chaz and I searching around for her. The following night we were on Master's feet again in front of the fire and later we curled up on his bed after we had 'Kissed' him goodnight. Master snored for most of the night but I slept through it, the bed was so warm and comfortable.

This routine continued for the next few days and we got used to it but it was all to change one day when a car arrived on the front gravel of the cottage. We had just got back from a long walk with Master and were asleep on the lawn. We ran around to the front just as Pat was getting out of the car. We gave her a huge greeting; it was lovely to see her back again. That night we were back into our normal beds, we didn't mind we were just so pleased that Pat was home.

The following morning after breakfast we were anxious to have our walk but Master and Pat sat and talked for ages, despite excited barks from Chaz. We were soon back to normal or as normal as things could be at 'Pandemonium' as we were taken for a walk later by Master and Pat.

# *The Boot*

A beautiful sunny breezy morning saw us on a long walk with Pat. She had taken us down a lane to a neighbouring farm where there were some interesting scents which we wanted to investigate but we were held firm on our leads. By the time we had returned to the cottage we were both exhausted. The sun had disappeared and clouds were rolling in. We slept on the lawn as the breeze increased.

Later that morning we both leapt to our feet when we heard footsteps on the gravel in front of the cottage. We ran around to investigate, Chaz was barking. We saw the postman standing at the front door talking to Master. The postman made a fuss of us after handing over a large package to Master. We followed the postman back to the gate and he made another fuss of us as he closed the gate behind him, he was a very nice man!

We went indoors as the rain began to fall. I watched with some interest as Master opened the package and he took out a shiny pair of black boots. I reached up and smelt them as he put them on the table, they smelt quite nice.

Later that day, Master polished the boots before putting them on and taking us for a walk along to the farm yard, and the orchard beyond, the rain had stopped and the ground smelt very fresh. That evening we settled down in front of the fire with Master and Pat. The fire was roaring away and the heat from it was beautiful. Once or twice it crackled loudly which startled both of us.

Pat settled us down in our beds at bedtime and gave us our little treat as she did every night, before saying "Goodnight you two" and turning off the light. In the gloom I noticed the new boots on the worktop; with my head on my feet I looked at them for ages before curiosity got the better of me. I went over to the boots, one of which had a lace that was hanging down. I gently pulled the lace and the boot fell off of the worktop and on to the floor, narrowly missing my front paws.

I carried it over to my bed, Chaz was snoring loudly. I began chewing at the leather on the back of the boot. It was pretty tough but didn't taste too bad. I chewed at it for ages before growing tired and sleeping with my new toy next to me. I awoke a few times during the night and chewed some more. By the morning I had managed to shred the back of the boot and ate some of the leather.

As usual Chaz began barking as daylight broke and Pat came down and let us out into the garden before feeding us. The boot was buried deep under the blankets in my bed. Later that morning Master drove out of the front gate in his uniform and we did not see him for the rest of the day. That evening I sat on Pat's feet as she made a fuss of me. Master returned quite late and we greeted him, before he put us to bed with a treat.

After the light was switched off I dug down in my blankets and found the boot. I chewed on it some more through the night. By the morning the whole back of the boot was shredded. Master took us for a walk in the rain that was very heavy and there was a strong wind blowing. Master was dressed up for the weather and had his Wellington boots on. We walked briskly around the fields with our eyes squinted against the driving rain.

We were soaked through when we got back and after Master had got out of all his clothes he dried us down with towels. He made a real fuss of us which we thoroughly enjoyed. He took ages to dry us off but eventually our coats were almost dry.

He then went over to our beds to shake them up for us and it was at that point that the remains of the boot appeared. Master just stood and stared at it for some time before he reached down and picked it up. I crept away with my ears down and my tail between my legs while Chaz simply went and curled up in her bed.

Master looked down at me and waved the boot at me angrily and said "What have you done you bad dog". I backed into the corner and looked away; I did not want to make eye contact with him. He approached me and waved the remains of the boot close to my face and shouted "You bad girl". It was obvious to me that I was in trouble, the tone and pitch of his voice said it all. He glared at me for ages as I looked away, I began to shake uncontrollably. He stormed out of the room carrying the boot and slammed the door behind him. I looked at Chaz as I crept into bed, but typically she was already asleep and oblivious to what had just gone on.

I could not sleep so I lay in my bed the rest of the day worried that I had upset Master. The rain continued and Pat let us out a couple of times but we did not see Master until late into the evening when Pat let us through to the sitting room where Master was sitting. I was pleased to see him and I crawled sheepishly over to him and sat on his feet and placed my muzzle in his lap to say "Sorry" but he totally ignored me. I eventually went over to Pat and she made a fuss of me.

Later Master put us to bed and we had our treats. He then sat on the step and made a fuss of both of us. He spoke at length to me, although I didn't understand a word he was saying it was obviously about the boot as I heard this word mentioned a few times, but the tone was a lot better, and he even managed a smile. He stroked me behind my ears which I loved and I licked his hands as he smiled at me and gave me a big hug. Chaz joined in the fussing and he gave us both a big hug before he put us to bed and turned out the light and said "Goodnight you two and sleep tight"

I slept very well that night with no dreams of giant boots!

# *Harry*

One morning Mac had arrived early and joined Pat and Master for breakfast. The smell of cooking coming from the kitchen was mouth watering. Mac did slip us some bacon rind from the table when the other two were not looking.

Chocka and Harry

Soon after breakfast we heard the sound of a car arriving on the gravel out front. Chaz and I ran around to investigate and we saw Phil and Sarah arriving. In their car was a Labrador and he was let out. He was a huge dog and we learnt that his name was 'Harry'. He greeted us and we sniffed each other all over, he was a good looking dog!

We followed him around the garden as he scent marked at various locations. He began to pay a lot of attention to us, particularly Chaz. We ran around the garden playing rough and tumble until we all collapsed on the patio in the sun.

He stayed with us all day but later he leapt into his car and we watched him leave. This was the first of regular meetings and play times we were to have with him. His scent lingered on the lawn for a long time.

# Builders

Soon after Harry's visit some builders moved in and began work on extending our room and building a glass room, which I later learnt was a conservatory, at the other end of the cottage. The builders were nice and spoilt us with their sandwiches when Master and Pat were not watching. We had to move out of our room for a while as the extension progressed. We didn't mind, it was more comfortable in the kitchen.

Eventually the tiles were laid in our new room which was a lot bigger. A washing machine and a tumble drier were installed and eventually our beds were moved back in. There were some interesting scents in there but we liked the extra space that we had.

Almost at the same time the conservatory was completed. This became a favourite room for us and for Master and Pat. It was lovely just laying on the floor in front of the doors in the sun, Chaz and I would challenge each other to get the best position in the mornings, I normally won.

# *A Long run*

Deer have always fascinated me although I have yet to get close to one. How do they manage to run so fast and for such vast distances? One incident with deer landed us in deep trouble with Master again!

It was winter time and the ground was very wet and soft after a lot of rain. We were out with Master on our morning walk. We were off the leads and walking by his side as good dogs should do. We were walking along the top of the orchard, when Chaz suddenly picked up the scent of something in the wet grass and disappeared through the hedge next to us. I followed. We were in a huge open field with a very low crop. Way off in the distance I could see a number of deer running away from us. Chaz had already spotted them and was running flat out, I joined her.

The field was very wet and there were some puddles in the crop. It made running difficult but the excitement of seeing the deer spurred us on. I could hear Master calling from behind the hedge but we ignored him. The scent on the ground was strong and the deer had left deep hoof marks in the mud.

On and on we went and Master's voice grew faint. The deer had disappeared through a hedge but their scent was strong. We reached the thin hedge and ran through at the point where the deer had gone. There was no sign of them on the other side so we followed the scent which led us straight to another field. It was beginning to rain which wasn't really any help. The mud was sticking to my paws and was weighing heavy on my legs but on we ran, although I began to sense that Chaz was beginning to tire. I always knew that I was fitter than her!

We passed through two more huge fields with the rain now really falling heavily and it was cold rain. The deer scent was now weak, possibly due to the rain. Chaz and I came to a stop in the middle of a field. We were covered in mud and were soaked with the rain and the water filled ditches that we had run through. We were both panting heavily. We sat there for quite a while just looking around.

All of a sudden we heard Master's voice way off in the distance and it soon became apparent that he was approaching. We saw him approaching through the heavy rain. His boots were covered in mud and he was struggling to walk. I could see that he was carrying our leads. Closer and closer he drew and the body language and the angry tone in his voice suggested to me that it was us that he was angry with but I couldn't understand why.

He was a very short distance from us when he said "what do you think you were doing you bad dogs" At that

Chaz ran off in the direction from whence we had come. I was not going to face his wrath on my own so I followed her. Master shouted angrily at us but we ignored him and ran. As we reached the hedge I looked back and saw Master walking back the direction that he had come. We followed our scent back to the orchard and we then knew our way home.

We were both shattered as we walked through the top gate which was open and back into the garden. We stood at the closed back door and Chaz gave out a bark. Pat opened the door, and smiled and said "well, where have you two been?" She saw the state we were in, so she came outside with a coat and boots on and we were hosed down on the gravel, and as she did Master came around the corner after parking his car up.

He said "I do not believe you two?" and walked off. Obviously we were not flavour of the month. As he was taking off his mud caked boots by the back door Pat said to him "At least they came home" what ever that meant, Master made no comment but just looked at us as the mud came off us. Pat dried us with towels and we slept for the rest of the day.

That night we eventually got up, albeit with some difficulty as we were both very stiff. We wandered into the sitting room where the fire was crackling away. Master looked at us and we at him. We both curled up on his feet and went back to sleep as he stroked us.

From that point on we wore leads on our walks except for one orchard that was completely fenced in, we could not escape or so Master and Pat thought!

# *Frankie*

One morning Master and Pat had taken us for an early morning walk and we were resting out on the lawn in the sun. I heard a car on the gravel in the front driveway and ran around to investigate. The car stopped and a man got out, he was one of the builders that had worked on the cottage. In the back of the car was a large handsome Labrador dog who was let out. He greeted both of us and we chased him around the garden. His name was 'Frankie'.

He began to pay a lot of attention to Chaz, it was her time of the year when she really fancied dogs; a fact not lost on Frankie. After running around for quite a while I went indoors and laid down, leaving the other two still running around, they were both getting very excited.

Suddenly I heard a loud yelp from outside; Master Pat and Frankie's Master ran outside shutting the back door behind them. They were gone for quite a while before Master brought Chaz back in. She was exhausted and Frankie's scent was all over her. She laid down next to me and I licked her face gently. We slept for the rest of the day and that evening Pat lit the fire. We did not see Frankie again that day.

Chaz and I curled up in front of the crackling logs; it was a nice place to be. Later we were put to bed by Pat who gave us our little treat and we got a little extra this night, before the light was turned out and she said “Goodnight” as the door closed. Chaz snored all night.

# Hares

Soon after Frankie's visit Chaz began to put on weight and I knew that she was going to produce some puppies, but that was a little way off yet. One morning we were out walking with Master, we were both on leads, it did not bother me but Chaz did not like it. We were walking around a large field on the farm; there were some interesting scents on the strong breeze. An unwary rabbit jumped out of the hedge ahead of us but on seeing us it jumped back in. Although I saw it Chaz didn't. We walked on.

The crop in the field was not very high and we could clearly see into it. Suddenly I saw two hares pop up in the field close to us, they began running and Chaz and I began running on our extending leads. By the time we reached the end of the leads we were at full speed. I felt a hard tug and our leads went loose and at the same time I felt and heard a loud thud on the ground, Master was flat on the ground behind us. He shouted angrily at us but we ignored him, again! We were in hot pursuit of the rapidly disappearing hares.

The crop we were running through was very wet and we were soon soaked and muddy. The hares had disappeared into the orchard but their scent was strong on the ground. We ran through the orchard with our leads bouncing along behind us. We ran through a hedge behind the orchard and as we did the handle of Chaz's lead somehow got stuck between two strong stems and she came to an abrupt halt. I ran on leaving Chaz struggling to free herself. She was twisting around and around which only served to tie her up even further in the hedge, her lead was wrapped around within the base of the hedge. I gave up the pursuit as the hares were long gone and returned to Chaz who was barking and yelping. I could see Master approaching through the orchard. He was covered from head to foot in mud and didn't look very happy!

I sat patiently as Master started to release the twisted and knotted lead. He had to get down on to his hands and knees and crawl into the hedge to unwind the lead. I went over and licked his face which he did not appreciate very much. It took Master ages to untangle the lead from the hedge and there were a lot of angry words as Chaz still struggled to get free which didn't help. Eventually the lead was free and Chaz was out. We walked home in silence and were hosed down on the patio, Master looked as if he needed hosing down as well? We kept out of the way for the rest of the day, that being the sensible thing to do. That evening we slept on Master's feet in front of the fire. From that day on we were always kept on short leads.

# *Puppies*

As the weeks went by after the incident with the hares and Chaz stuck in the hedge, she began to put on a lot of weight. Our daily walks became shorter as she soon became tired and would sit down on the ground and rest. Eventually I was walked on my own for a while as Chaz would spend most of the day sleeping.

Then one morning our lives were changed for ever. Chaz had been very restless during the early part of the night after Pat had put us to bed. She was pacing up and down and then laying down on her bed next to me. Then in the early hours of the morning it started. She was laid out next to me when she began pushing and shortly after, a tiny black bundle appeared in the bed behind her. She turned around and licked it and I could see that it was moving; and it gave out a little cough. I got up and sniffed it gently while Chaz was still licking the little bundle which of course was a puppy.

Shortly after, Chaz began pushing again and then another puppy appeared in the bed and she began licking

Chaz with newborn pups

Chaz and Milk Bar

Chip at 10 days old

that one with my help. At that point Pat came into the room and on seeing the puppies immediately called Master, who quickly arrived. They spoke excitedly as they looked down at the new arrivals. Pat made a big fuss of me as I sat and watched the puppies. Pat disappeared shortly and when she returned Chaz was pushing again and as we all watched a third puppy appeared.

Master took me for a walk around the farm; it seemed strange not having Chaz by my side. When we returned Chaz was curled up with her tiny babies suckling milk from her. I sat down nearby and watched with Pat and Master. Throughout that day people came and went having seen the new arrivals. The following night Chaz slept deeply but I kept on waking up and checking her new family. There were two bitch pups and one dog.

Chaz was a good mother and for the first few days would not leave the puppies apart from quickly going into the garden to do her toilet. I stayed with them as well apart from the walks; I missed Chaz's company. The puppies grew well on Chaz's milk and soon had their eyes open and began to move around in the pen in the bedroom that had been built in our room for them. With the puppies safely contained Chaz again joined me on the walks but she was always anxious to return to her little family.

A low gate was placed across the back door and the puppies would jump up and look out at the great wide world beyond. A large pen was built on the lawn and one morning after our walk the puppies were gathered up and brought outside and placed in the pen, Chaz hopped in but I was happy to watch them through the wire mesh. They were not at all interested in suckling when Chaz laid down they were too busy investigating the grass. A shade was put up over the pen to protect the pups from the strong sunlight.

This became a daily routine and the puppies grew stronger and stronger. They would chase each other around in the pen, grabbing each other's tails and jumping over each other until they were worn out, then they would flake out on the grass. I would sit outside the pen watching and sometimes they would jump up with their front paws resting on the top of the pen and I would lick them. Pat fenced off all the flower beds in the garden and the pond, for although we knew that they were 'no go' areas, the puppies didn't.

One morning Pat and Master lifted the puppies out of the pen and the real fun began. Chaz and I followed them around as they investigated everywhere. Eventually however they got bored with this and turned their attentions to Chaz and I. They began chasing us around the garden and of course I let them catch me. They climbed all over me, pulling my tail and my ears until I jumped up with a sudden leap and the puppies would roll over in the grass and another chase would follow, ending up with them all over me again. Eventually the puppies would lay down exhausted and so did I, but the rest was not for long before they wanted more chasing and rough and tumble. This became the daily routine and was great fun, I loved the pups.

Pups Chip on right

Christmas is coming

Double Trouble

# *Frankie visits his Pups*

It was about this time when Frankie paid a visit. The pups greeted him with an air of curiosity and he was not too sure about them. With the initial reservations out of the way they began a rough and tumble with their dad, he thoroughly enjoyed their company although they soon wore him out. He would lay down to rest, panting heavily until the pups pounced on him again. He would leap up and chase them around the garden and the rose bed in the middle. Sometimes they would cheat and run straight through the middle of the rose bed to catch Frankie, he would then fall over and let them pile in on top of him.

Chaz and I would sit and watch as the games went on for most of the day; the puppies had boundless energy and were full of mischief. By the end of the day poor old Frankie was absolutely shattered and still the pups wanted more. I think that Frankie was quite relieved when his Master appeared. He needed little encouragement to jump up into his Master's van. The pups slept well that night.

.

I loved playing with them while Chaz slept. With three hungry appetites to satisfy it was draining her energy and she slept a lot of the time. As time went by the puppies turned their attention more and more to me. As they grew so did their teeth and it began to hurt when they grabbed my ears so I had to put an end to that. It was a lovely summer with the puppies as I watched them grow into young adults.

In the late summer one of the bitch puppies was collected by a couple and soon after the dog also went, this left one bitch puppy. But this was not the last we saw of them, for sometime later they visited us again.

Frankie, A proud Dad

Chip

# 'Chip'

The last remaining puppy was named 'Chip' by Master and Pat. She missed her brother and sister, but with us two around she was soon playing with us, and they became a distant memory. We would spend ages chasing around the garden, she was very fit and fast. After a good run around Chaz and I would collapse on the grass panting for air. Chip would pounce on us to play more and she would poke us with her paw. She had boundless energy and she was lovely.

The rough and tumbles got rougher, the tumbles felt harder and I had to put her in her place more than once. She would regularly pin me to the ground by my throat, not hard of course but I let her think that she had me! Eventually I would leap up and pin her down the same way. She would also run around the garden with us in hot pursuit, I could in fact out run her but I let her lead. She would sometimes turn in full flight and run between us. We soon cottoned on to this and when she tried to run back we would close ranks like a pincer movement and grab her.

She still had to learn where the 'no go' areas were in the garden and it took her quite a while. She would sometimes cheat when we were chasing her and she would run straight through one of the flower beds, and we would hear Pat shout "No". Chip eventually learnt that we were not allowed on to any of the flower beds but it took a lot of shouting from Pat.

At night Chip would leap between or on top of us. Chaz would often dream a lot and was very restless at night and Chip learnt to snuggle up to me.

In our room there was a line of coats hanging up and although they were in our reach we had never bothered with them. One evening Chip began to tug at a pocket on one of the coats which was Master's, he didn't wear it very often. She began to chew at the material which eventually ripped and a cascade of doggy treats fell on to our bed. That was what she was after! She began to eat them and we helped her, well there was no point not seizing on the opportunity. The treats were pretty stale but they all went.

Soon after, Master came in and noticed the torn remains of the coat and the pocket - Chip had done a good job. He looked down at all three of us. Fortunately Chip still had some material around her mouth. He held her by the scruff of the neck up to the pocket and said "What is this?" Her tail and ears went down as she looked up at Master. He was very angry. He shouted at her "What is this Chip, you bad dog" Chaz and I kept well out of the way. Master looked around at us two and said "I don't suppose you two had anything to do with this?" We looked at him; boy was it nice to have a scapegoat for a change. Pat came in and looked at the coat or should I say the remains of it.

Pat took the coat off the hook and walked out of the room with Master, the door was firmly shut behind them. I could hear Master and Pat talking and I heard Chip's name mentioned a number of times and laughter from both of them.

Later that night all three of us slept on Master and Pat's feet as usual. Chip was now one of the family.

Can I have a go?

# Chaz has an operation

Early one morning we had had our breakfast and a short run around the fields after which, Chip and I were shut in our room by Master and shortly after we heard a car leaving the front drive and the gate close. Master came in and we were let out. We both ran around to the front but there was a car missing and there was no sign of Chaz. We searched high and low around the garden and the cottage but there was no sign of her. Chip began to pine for her but I started a game with her on the lawn, chasing each other and having a good rough and tumble.

I heard the sound of a car on the gravel out front and we both ran around to investigate. It was Pat and there was no sign of Chaz. Master and Pat sat on the patio for sometime talking before our collars and leads were put back on and we went for another walk but this time we went a lot further around the farm and the reservoir where there were two huge white birds sitting on the water in the middle. We wanted to go and investigate but were held firm. Master told me that they were "Swans" and "That they could hurt you". Whatever that meant I did not know but the firmness of the lead suggested that we would not be allowed to go into the water and see them. The bird's eyes were fixed on us throughout our walk around the top of the reservoir.

Back home Chip and I slept on the grass and I dreamt of giant Swans! Late afternoon Pat drove out in the car and Master shut the gate before we could follow. A few minutes later she was back and Chaz was in the back with a huge lampshade over her head which I recognised immediately. As she was lifted out of the car, Chip greeted her and Pat told her to be "Gentle". Chaz was very subdued and appeared groggy. We followed her into the cottage. She banged the collar on the doorway and on a chair which jolted her head. She laid down on her bed and slept. Chip and I kept her company. I sniffed at her tummy and could see a number of stitches there. She had a very restless night; she could not get comfortable with the collar on.

The following morning Chaz had difficulty eating her breakfast because of the collar but like me she learnt that if she pressed down firmly on the collar she could reach the bowl. She came outside, banging the collar on the back door post as she came out. She laid down on the lawn. Chip tried to get her to play but she was not interested so I played with Chip until I was worn out.

This was the routine for the next few days and slowly Chaz's energy returned. She was running around the garden with the collar on or should I say what was left of it. She had banged it so many times that the plastic was shattered. One morning Pat and Master looked at Chaz's stitches and Pat very carefully removed the stitches while Chip and I sat nearby and watched. Chip wanted to go in and investigate but Master held her firm. Chaz laid perfectly still as the stitches came out without any difficulty and the remains of the collar were removed.

Within a few days Chaz was back to her old self.

# *'Tinks' and 'Henry's' visit*

Chip was about a year old when two visitors arrived one sunny afternoon. We had had our walk with Pat and were basking in the summer sun on the lawn, when I heard a car arrive on the gravel at the front of the cottage. Chip and I ran around to investigate, Chaz was sound asleep. Two people had arrived who I vaguely recognised but it was not until they let their black Labrador out of the back that I remembered who they were. They were the couple who collected Chip's sister last year and the dog that had jumped out of the car was the very dog. I soon learnt that her name was 'Tinks' and she had grown into a fine dog. We greeted each other and both Chip and I recognised her scent and she ours.

She ran around to the back of the cottage where she met her mum who had just woken up, they greeted each other with some gusto; it was obvious that they recognised each other. Soon all four of us were belting around the garden and having a really good rough and tumble, just like the old days. Tinks was to stay with us for a few days and we had great fun both in the garden and out on the walks. In the orchard with the fence around it we were all off our leads and were running around chasing each other through the trees. Chaz became a little over protective towards Tinks and if she felt that Chip was getting a little too rough with her she would step in and separate them. Even I was given a warning one day when Tinks and I were having a rough and tumble, Chaz thought I was being too rough with Tinks but in reality it was the other way round, she was a powerful dog even at one year old.

Eventually, Tinks was collected and returned to her home but we were to see her again from time to time.

A short while after Tinks had gone, early one morning another car arrived on the gravel and we ran around to investigate. A lady got out and two black Labradors were let out of the back. We greeted each other and I realised from the scent of one of them that it was Chip's brother. We soon learnt that his name was 'Henry' and the other dog was a dog called 'Harry' which confused me a bit, as I knew Harry as being the yellow dog owned by Phil and Sarah. The confusion didn't last long. We had a good run around the garden and the inevitable rough and tumble that lasted ages.

While we were outside we had not noticed that a huge double bed had arrived in our room and the lady had gone. The rest of the day was all thrills and spills around the garden. Once or twice George and Henry were shouted at by Pat as they ran through her flower beds; they soon learnt that this was a 'No Go' area. That night we all eventually settled down on our beds. Chaz did try and take over the double bed but she was out numbered. We were all pretty tired and we all slept well although Henry was dreaming a lot; it must be a family trait because Chip tends to dream a lot. I used to when I was younger but as I have got older I dream less frequently.

The following morning Pat and Master came down early and gave us our food. Henry and George had theirs outside to prevent us, and in particular Chaz, from eating theirs as well. We were given a short walk before we began playing in the garden. Chip took on the two 'Guests' and gave them a good run for their money and it was not long before they were collapsed on the lawn with their tongues hanging out and panting like mad. This was the pattern for the rest of the day, with Chaz and I joining in with short bursts of energy before collapsing in heaps. We all slept very well the following night.

Early the following morning a car arrived on the front gravel, it was the lady with our guests who were bundled into the back of the car with their bed, bowls and leads. We all sat and watched as the car left the drive; Henry and George were looking at us out of the back of the car. Their scent remained on the lawn for quite a few days until the rain came.

# 'Brodie'

Soon after the coat incident, work began on the construction of a new garage to the side of the cottage. A tractor digger worked for two days digging deep holes and trenches in the ground. We wanted to investigate but we were not allowed there.

One morning a large van arrived and a man got out and went to a side door on the van which slid open. There standing in the doorway was a real giant of a dog. He was black and brown and had a long shaggy coat. We soon learnt that his name was Brodie. He leapt out of the van and towered over us three. I think he was the largest dog that I had ever seen. He greeted us and then began a gentle trot around the garden; we were running flat out to keep up with him he was a real giant of a dog.

Chip took a real shine to him and they played on the lawn. He was so big that she could run underneath him. When he laid down she would jump all over him and he would simply place one paw very gently onto her and hold her down until she struggled free and leapt all over him again. He was a gentle giant.

Over the next few months Brodie became a regular visitor and a good friend to all of us but in particular Chip. They would play for hours on the lawn.

# The Vets!

Although I would never play up at the vets I did not like them at all. Early one morning after a quick walk with Pat around the reservoir, where Chaz wanted to go for a swim but she was not allowed, we were bundled into the car. As usual Chaz needed help to get in.

We left the cottage and after a short drive we were jumping out of the car on our leads. The air was full of scent particularly on the grass around the car park. I recognised the place, we had been here before. Eventually we were led into the building and a waiting room. There were two people sitting there. One was holding a lead attached to a very old Labrador who was stretched out on the floor. Chip tried to go over and say "Hello" but she was held firm by Master. A lady was sitting nearby with a cage on her lap and there was a strong scent of rabbit coming from it. Chaz pulled hard on her lead to investigate the cage but Pat held her firm. We were told to "Sit" and we did; encouraged of course with a little treat!

After quite a long wait during which time Chip became very restless, we were led into a room where the vet was standing. We were told to sit and we did. Chip was lifted up onto the table and the vet checked her over. We heard a little yelp from her as she received an injection. She was lowered down and sat next to me and Chaz was lifted up by Master and the vet, she was struggling - like me, she didn't like the vets. After her examination she was returned to the floor where the vet proceeded to cut her nails which she really did not like and she made quite a fuss, but it was soon over.

After that it was my turn, there was little point struggling. I was poked and prodded all over; I could have told the vet that there was nothing wrong with me. I felt a sharp prick in the back of my neck which only lasted a second or so. Shortly after I was back on the ground and we were being led out and back to the car. I was quite relieved to be jumping back in but Master had to help Chaz in. I really do not know why she can not leap in like Chip and I do?

We were soon basking in the sun on our lawn.

# *Wasps!*

It was the time of the year when there was plenty of fruit on the ground in the orchard and it was great fun for the three of us. Now this particular year we had experienced a lot of wasps in the garden and having been stung when I was on the streets of Saffron Walden, I did not like them. In fact I had a thing about flies generally, which probably went back to the days when I was rummaging around dustbins.

One morning Pat was taking us for a walk through the two orchards and Chaz and I were munching into the sweet apples on the ground. I had just bitten in to one when I felt a sharp pain in my lip, I yelped as it stung me again before I was able to get rid of it. At the same time I heard Chaz give out a loud yelp. My lip began to swell but I was determined to get another apple. We walked on to the second orchard with a fence around it and Pat let us off our leads.

There were plenty of beautiful sweet plums on the ground and Chaz and I were soon tucking in. Suddenly I felt another painful sting in my other lip and almost at the same time a further sting in my top jaw. I yelped in pain.

Soon after Chaz yelped, and Pat called us in and our leads were put back on, we were led out of the orchard. On the way home my lips became very swollen and my jaw was throbbing. When Chaz and I were back in the garden and we had had our treat, we rubbed our jaws on the grass to relieve the pain. It was a long time before the pain and swelling subsided.

I do not like Wasps!!

# *New Recruits?*

One morning we were out walking with Master around a big field on the farm; by the pace that he was walking he was obviously in a hurry. Chip was off the lead and Chaz and I were on very short leads. I think that Master was working on the theory that with us two on leads Chip would not run off!

We were passing a hedge when we reached a gap. Chip suddenly spotted something in the field and stood alert with her ears forward. We knew immediately that she was on to something so we dragged Master over to the gap. As we reached the gap, Chip was off like lightening which appeared to catch Master unawares. We wanted to follow and ran and jolted Master's hands and he lost grip of both leads; we were off at full speed across the field behind the hedge after a small deer that was way ahead of Chip who was running flat out. I could hear Master calling behind us but this was more fun. We soon crossed that field and caught up with Chip at the hedge. She had lost the scent but not for long due to the trusted nose of Chaz. We were back on the scent in the next field, we had lost sight of the deer but the scent was strong in the wet sticky ground.

We skirted around the big farm house and eventually found ourselves in the wood where the scent trail became a little confusing as there were scents crisscrossing everywhere. We continued running through the wood albeit a little slower, then through a muddy water filled ditch on the other side. We had lost the scent and eventually found ourselves back on the road where we had been before. We trotted down the road with mud and water dripping off us, and our leads dragging along behind.

We reached the driveway where the men in uniform were standing and we walked up to the barrier where the two men were. One of the men looked at us and said "Now what do we have here?" At that point another man in uniform approached us from a nearby building and said

"Not you two again and who is the newcomer?" He led us into the building where we had been before, there were a number of men and women in uniform. We were offered a bowl of water which we soon emptied, chasing after deer is thirsty work. A lady came up to us and gave us some biscuits, she was very nice!

We sat down on the floor, we were all exhausted. We must have looked a motley crew. We watched as people came and went. They were all in uniform and were wearing caps. It was nice and warm in there and I dropped off to sleep for a while.

Suddenly I heard a voice outside that I recognised, it was Master. The door eventually opened and in he came with another man in uniform but he was wearing a cap. Master took one look at the three of us and then spoke to the man. He said "I am sorry for this and thank you for taking them in". The man smiled and said "No problem." Master grabbed our leads and we were led out to his car which was parked nearby. We were put in the back, of course Chaz needed help. Master did not say a word to us but his body language said it all; we were in the 'Dog house' again.

As we drove out and on to the road he broke his silence and said "I am fed up with all three of you" That was all he said as we drove back to the cottage, where Pat was waiting with the hose. We knew what was coming next. Pat gave us quite a lecture and although I did not understand what she was saying, the tone was enough. After our wash we were dried off with towels before going to bed where we stayed for the rest of the day. Master disappeared in his uniform and did not return till late in the evening.

He came in and sat down in his usual chair in the sitting room in front of the fire. All three of us had been sleeping on Pat's feet and I moved over to Master's feet and made my peace with him, the others followed.

We were all quite stiff after the day's excitement, but I can't think why!

# *Harry's bed*

Early one morning Master and Pat took us for a long walk, but all three of us were on tight leads, this was the new system, which none of us liked very much. I had overheard Master talking to Pat about the "Pack instinct with a number of dogs" I didn't know what it meant, all I knew was that I liked running. Still it seemed as if those days were over, or so I thought!

We were asleep on the lawn at the back of the cottage when I heard a car on the gravel out the front. We all ran around to investigate. Phil and Sarah had arrived who were regular visitors to Pandemonium. They had brought Harry with them, he jumped out of the back of the car and greeted us three, then ran around the back garden with us in hot pursuit.

We played chase with him, racing at full speed around our large garden and then he would chase us. He was continually scent marking everywhere. Phil and Sarah were sitting with Master and Pat on the patio watching us and laughing. We were so busy playing with Harry we did not see Phil and Sarah leave. Eventually, totally exhausted we all came into our room where a new bed had appeared, and it was full of Harry's scent. Before he had a chance to lay down on it, Chaz was there, stretched out on the bed. Every time Harry went to lay on it Chaz would growl a warning. Eventually Harry came and laid with Chip and I.

Later Pat came in and saw Chaz spread out on Harry's bed. She removed her from the bed and beckoned Harry over on to it. Chaz reluctantly came and lay down with us. Chaz was not happy. As soon as Pat left the room Chaz got up and went over to Harry and growled a warning at him. Harry got off his bed and rejoined us. Chaz spread out on the bed, victorious, or so she thought! Pat returned a little while later and removed Chaz again but this time with a very stern warning; but as soon as Pat was gone Harry was ousted from his bed and Chaz snuggled down again. I do not know why Chaz liked Harry's bed so much, it was no better than ours!

Prior to Master and Pat going to bed they came in to say goodnight as usual. Pat saw Chaz on Harry's bed and scolded her. Harry's bed was removed from our room and was spread out in the room next door. Harry snuggled down on his bed as the door was shut between the two rooms. I could hear him snoring through the door.

As soon as the door opened the following morning Harry joined us for breakfast. We were soon racing around the garden. Our collars were put on later and we went for a long walk around the farm. Chaz and Harry went for a swim in the reservoir. Harry was a powerful swimmer and collected the stick every time Master threw it, but much to the annoyance of Chaz, who was no mean swimmer herself. When we got home Chaz and Harry were dried off on towels before Chaz snuggled down on Harry's bed. He slept with us in the sun on the lawn.

Later that day Phil and Sarah collected Harry and his bed!

# *Chip in hospital*

Early one morning Master took us for a walk and judging by his pace he was in a hurry. When we returned home, Pat called Chip indoors and the door was shut. A few minutes later the door reopened and Master was standing in the doorway. I went between his legs to see my mate but she was not there. I searched the cottage but couldn't find her. I ran outside, followed by Chaz. We went around the front and I found Chip's fresh scent on the gravel and there was only one car in the garage.

I began to panic and searched the garden for her but she was no where to be found. I went and sat with Master on the patio. I sat on his feet and cried; he stroked me and said "Don't worry Chocka she will be back soon". Pat returned and I greeted her when she got out of the car and I expected to see Chip, she wasn't in the car, where was she? I was tense for the rest of the day. I couldn't rest. I patrolled the garden and the front yard, desperately looking for my little pal. Chaz on the other hand was not at all perturbed by the disappearance of her little daughter; she just slept on and off all day.

That night I was very restless, I missed having my pal lying next to me. Even Chaz was growing a little anxious. Early the following morning Master took us for a walk. I didn't enjoy it, I kept looking behind expecting to see Chip but she was nowhere to be seen. When we got back there was no sign of Pat and a car was missing. Master was sitting on the patio when we heard the sound of a car on the gravel. Chaz and I ran around to the front, it was Pat. She got out of the car, shut the gate leading to the road and opened the back door of the car and out jumped my pal. She was very subdued and had a huge plastic lampshade on her head again this I recognised. We greeted her enthusiastically and Pat said "Gently, you two". I could see that Chip had rows of tiny white stitches in her eye lids. I went to lick them but Pat grabbed me and said very firmly "No", I understood that.

Poor Chip was not happy with the collar on her head; she kept on crashing into things, particularly in the cottage. Gaps between the beams and the furniture that she could normally get through were now impossible with the collar on; she would be stopped in her tracks with a jolt. I stuck close to her as she trotted around the garden; it was nice to have her back. She laid down on the lawn and we laid either side of her. She slept for the rest of the day. That night after we were put to bed and the lights were turned out, Chaz very gently licked Chip's eyes for a while before we all settled down for the night. Chip was restless; she could not get comfortable with the collar on. She woke up a number of times crying, I would comfort her as best I could.

Life was difficult for the next few days for Chip but she slowly adjusted to the collar and the restrictions that it created. Her eyes soon healed. One morning Chip and Pat disappeared early in the car. I sat in the yard and watched the car leave with Chip looking out of the back window with her head surrounded by the collar. I laid down on the gravel in the sun looking at the gate. It was not long before the car was back at the gate and Pat was opening it. Chip eventually jumped out without the collar or the stitches, she was a lot happier.

We were soon racing around the garden and playing rough and tumble as if nothing had ever happened.

# *Rats!*

With the huge garden that we could play in and the river at the bottom of it, and the big open fields beyond and all around it, it was inevitable that we would get wildlife in the garden. We knew that foxes regularly visited us, especially in the winter, and the odd rabbit would risk life and limb to come into the garden. Soon after we arrived at the cottage, Chaz and I had detected the strong scent of rats in the garden and in particular around the areas of the green house and the rockery behind the pond. Chaz and I had chased them from time to time and in fact Chaz had caught and killed one, then she'd buried it under the hedge at the front of the cottage.

One winter's night it was cold and frosty. Master and Pat had let us out for our last toilet before bed. The night was still, there was no breeze. All three of us ran down the lawn but were brought up short when the still cold night air was shattered by a loud screech coming from near the greenhouse. I looked over and saw a huge rat hanging limp in the talons of an Owl which flew away on silent wings. It disappeared around the front of the cottage and away into the night.

A few days after the owl incident, snow arrived which gave us a lot of fun running through it with noses down, and Chip and I would play fight in the snow, rolling over and over while Chaz stood and barked nearby before joining in the rough and tumble.

Suddenly Chip went racing off across the snow and disappeared around by the greenhouse. Chaz and I followed rather curious as to what had attracted her attention. Just as we reached the greenhouse, Chip appeared from around the back, proudly holding the lifeless form of a huge rat in her jaws. Its head hung out one side and its tail was dragging along the ground out the other side. We followed her as she proudly carried it indoors, and laid down on her bed with it. I don't think she knew what to do with it.

Master appeared shortly after and as soon as he saw Chip with her prize he called Pat. They tried to get the rat off her but she was having none of that. The treats then appeared and we all got one. Chip had to put her prize down to eat her treat and Master managed to whisk it away without her seeing. She had soon forgotten all about it.

A few weeks later Chaz was around the back of the greenhouse near one of the compost bins, she had obviously disturbed something as she was barking excitedly. As Chip and I went to investigate a rat suddenly appeared running flat out with Chaz in hot pursuit barking loudly. We joined in the pursuit but the rat was really fast. It ran down the garden with Chip gaining on it, until it reached the bottom where it scaled one of the wooden fence posts and leapt into the long grass on the other side where we were not allowed. Master and Pat called it the 'Nature reserve' whatever that meant? All three of us ran along the bottom of the fence trying to find a way through but there were none. Master and Pat had come out of the cottage on hearing the commotion and we were called back to them where we were given a treat each.

That particular winter brought in a lot of rats to the garden and we spent a lot of time chasing them, it was great fun. Chip managed to catch one or two which she brought in but only to have them removed by Master or Pat, but it was good because it meant that we all got a treat!

# *Locked Up!*

Early one morning Pat took us for an early morning walk around the farm and it was the start of a very interesting day. When we got back we stretched out on the lawn in the sun while Pat and Master sat and talked on the patio. After a while they began work in the garden, we watched on in the shade of a tree, it was getting quite hot.

Later that day Phil, Sarah and Harry arrived. We greeted Harry and we chased each other around the garden until we all collapsed in a heap on the lawn. A short while later our collars were put on and we went for a walk with Harry. Pat was holding Chip, and Master had me and Chaz and Phil and Sarah had Harry. We walked up to the reservoir where Harry was released from his lead and he leapt into the water with a huge splash. Chaz was pulling really hard on her lead to join him. I heard Master say to Pat "It will be alright, they can't get into any trouble here". All our leads were released and Chaz leapt in, while Chip and I had a paddle in the shallows.

Pat threw a stick for Chaz and Harry and they swam for it. Harry reached it first and began to swim to shore with it. Chaz latched on to it so they were swimming side by side when they reached the shallows. Harry brought the stick to Master with Chaz still holding on to it. Chaz let go and shook herself right next to Master, who got showered. He was not best pleased. Pat threw the stick in again and side by side Chaz and Harry leapt off the bank and crashed into the water with a huge splash. The stick was way out and both dogs swam hard to reach it but Harry reached it first. As he turned to return with it, Chaz latched onto it again and side by side they swam back.

The stick was brought to Master who stood back this time as Chaz shook herself. As we stood there waiting for someone to throw the stick again, suddenly Chaz had picked up the scent of something in the field and she was off. Before Master or Pat had time to put our leads back on, Chip and I were in hot pursuit of Chaz who was rapidly disappearing in the crop. I could hear Master and Pat calling and blowing a whistle but we ignored them this was much more fun. Harry had not joined us on our little adventure.

We had soon caught up with Chaz who was on a strong deer scent. All three of us were running alongside each other, this was great. There was a strong breeze blowing, which we were running into; it was making our ears stand up. On and on we ran through several fields, hedges and muddy ditches; we had had heavy rain recently. We circled around some farm buildings and a small copse of trees where Chip got distracted by a squirrel which she chased until it disappeared up a tree. She was soon running alongside us as we found ourselves in a huge field with a road running alongside a hedge on the other side. We appeared to be close to Thaxted.

The heat and all the running was beginning to take it's toll on us and our run was reduced to a trot as the scent was fading. We had no idea where we were, this was new territory for us. We eventually reached the hedge and found a hole where we could get through. On the other side we found ourselves on a wide grass verge before a road where cars and Lorries were passing by. I did not like traffic; it made me nervous, probably a throw back to my younger days.

We sat watching the traffic for some time before Chaz made a move. She walked into the middle of the road and sat down. Chip joined her and reluctantly I did. I saw a car approach and slow down when it reached us. At the same time a huge lorry was bearing down on us from the opposite direction, it also slowed down and stopped. A loud 'whooshing' sound came from the lorry as it stopped which made me jump. I could see other cars stopping from both directions. We were too tired to move.

A lady got out of the front car and approached us at the same time the lorry driver got out. The lady said "Now where have you three come from?" She checked for our collars but they had been removed when our leads were taken off at the reservoir. The lorry driver spoke to the lady and returned to his cab only to return shortly after with some string. The string was placed around each of our necks and we were led to the lady's car. There was now a long queue of cars behind her car and a number of drivers were getting out and looking in our direction. The lady opened the back of her car and we were beckoned in. Chip and I managed to summon up the energy to jump in but Chaz couldn't so the lorry driver wrapped his huge arms around her and lifted her in.

As we drove off towards Thaxted at the top of the hill, I looked out of the back window as the long tail back of traffic began to move off. As we passed through Thaxted I laid down with the others as the lady spoke to us softly. We eventually stopped outside a big building, and the lady got out and disappeared inside. She came out shortly after with another woman who was wearing a uniform like Master's, the back door was opened and the woman from the building said "I think I know whose dogs these are". She helped us out of the car and we were led into the building and through to a little dark room with a concrete floor and a simple bed in one corner. A bowl of water was brought in and the big steel door was slammed shut, it echoed in the room. None of us liked this room and we curled up in a corner on the cold floor.

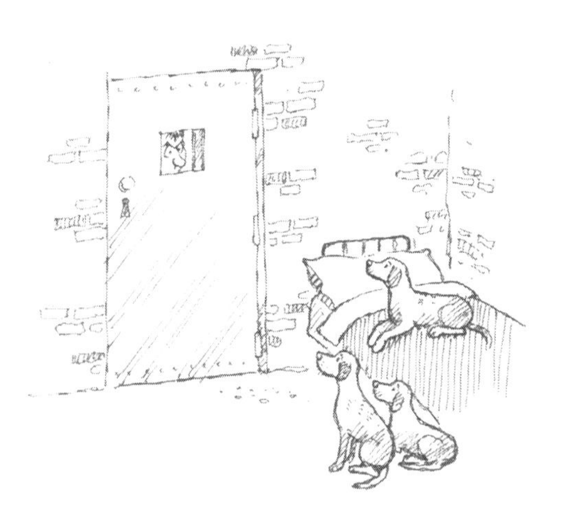

I later heard a sliding sound coming from the door and looked up to see that there was a face looking at us from an opening in the door and as I looked the opening slammed shut. It was much later that we heard the door being opened and there stood Master and Phil, were we relieved to see them again. Master walked in and said "Hopefully some time in the cell might have knocked some sense into you, you bad dogs".As usual I had not got a clue what he was saying but the tone was enough. We were led out and the lady said "Goodbye" as we left the station. We were bundled into the car, Chaz with help as usual and we drove off. Phil and Master were talking in the front; Master did not speak to us.

Back at the cottage we were hosed down and dried with towels without a word being spoken by anyone, the body language from Master in particular was enough. Phil and Sarah left with Harry and we went straight to bed and slept for ages. We were all very stiff the following morning. Pat took us for a short walk as Master had left early in uniform. That night we slept on Master and Pat's feet in the sitting room, but it was a few days before Master made a fuss of us, I think it was the longest he remained angry at us, and I for one didn't like it. It really upset me if I was in his bad books.

# 'Daisy' and 'Beth'

It was Christmas time and the tree had arrived in the conservatory and was covered with sparkling things and lights, by Pat. I sat and watched her for ages. People began coming and going, Mac was a regular visitor. Beccy and Ian called and had a meal and Phil, Sarah, Gina and Stuart also called for a meal, unfortunately Phil and Sarah didn't bring Harry. Other people came and went as the days went by.

One afternoon a car arrived on the gravel and we went to investigate. It was a lady we knew as Sue. She got out of her car and we greeted her. I then noticed two dogs in the back of the car and after Master shut the gate they were let out. They were both yellow Labradors. We soon learnt that their names were Daisy, who was a young bitch, and Beth who like Chaz and I, had seen quite a few Christmases.

We were soon around the back, Chaz was sitting on the patio with Beth and barking at us as Chip and I ran around the garden after Daisy, she was full of fun. We had a good rough and tumble on the lawn, despite the rain. We were covered in mud from the lawn but it soon dried in the warmth of the cottage. Two new beds had arrived in our

Daisy and Beth (foreground)

room and Chaz was soon spread out on one of them, which from the scent coming from it, belonged to Daisy. She didn't mind she curled up with Chip and I.

We heard a number of cars arriving on the front gravel but we couldn't go and investigate as we were shut in. We heard voices coming from within the cottage and eventually we were allowed through. There were people everywhere. After greeting everybody and getting a little treat from Master and Pat we went back to bed, as everybody sat around the dining table. There were some delicious scents coming from the kitchen.

Much later we heard the chinking of glasses and singing coming from the sitting room. At the same time I could hear the sound of the bells ringing across the fields from Thaxted church. In the distance I heard bangers going off, I for one did not like them, but they didn't last long. Master, Pat and Sue came in and said "Happy New Year, you lot" I didn't know what it meant but by the tone it was something good. I enjoyed the little treat that we were given.

We heard the cars going later and Master came in and said "Goodnight" and turned the light off. As soon as the door shut Chaz got up off of her bed and went over to Beth and barked at her, she wanted her bed but Beth was having none of it. Chaz also tried to move Daisy but she would not budge either, so Chaz came back to her bed and dropped on to it with a long sigh. Eventually Chaz and Beth were snoring well and Daisy was dreaming. Chip and I tried to ignore all the noise.

Pat came in early the following morning and let us out into the garden. After our breakfast, we had our collars put on and we all went for a walk. Sue had Beth, Master had Daisy and Chip and Pat had Chaz and I. We walked around the orchard and up to the reservoir where Chaz had a swim with Daisy. A pair of ducks took off from the water and I watched them disappear.

Back at home Chaz and Daisy were dried off with towels. Daisy and Beth were placed in Sue's car, without any help, maybe Chaz could learn something from them! They then left. We were to see them again on a number of occasions in the future.

# *Mac's little treats*

Early one morning, Master gave us an early walk and by the pace that we were walking he was obviously in a hurry for something. Soon after we got back we heard a car arrive on the front gravel. We raced around to investigate and we saw Mac getting out of his car. We welcomed him in our usual way; Chip almost knocked him over in her excitement.

Soon after Mac had arrived Master and Pat said "Goodbye" to us and told us to be "Good girls" They drove out of the front yard and Mac closed the gate behind them and returned to the cottage, we stayed close to him.

Later that morning we followed Mac out on to the patio, he had a cup in his hand and a packet which I sniffed, it smelt good. He sat down and began to eat biscuits from the packet. We sat around him looking at him and patiently waited. Eventually our patience was rewarded and he gave us a biscuit each, which we gently took from his hand. We waited for another which soon came. Mac then went to sleep so we stretched out on the lawn in the sun.

At lunch time Mac carried a tray out onto the patio and we followed him. He gave us each a piece of cheese to eat before disappearing back into the cottage. I later went in to see where Mac was and found him sound asleep in an armchair in the sitting room. Chip and I played on the lawn.

Later that afternoon Mac reappeared on the patio with a cup in his hand and the familiar packet in the other. He sat down and we gathered around and patiently looked at him. It was not long before the biscuits came our way and we sat and enjoyed three biscuits each.

Later that day Master and Pat returned and Mac left. This happened more and more as Pat and Master spent days away. We enjoyed it as Mac continued to spoil his "Girls" which was what he would call us.

We did like Mac!

# *Shut Out*

One evening all three of us were sitting in front of the fire with Pat, Master was out as usual. I heard a vehicle drive in on the gravel and recognised it as Master's, his big vehicle made a very distinctive sound. I ran to the front door and greeted him when he came in. He was bringing some bits in from his vehicle. It was pouring down with rain. I sneaked out to answer the call of nature and when I came back around to the front, Master's car was in the garage and there was no sign of him and the front door was firmly shut.

I ran around the back but the back door was also shut. I scratched at the door but it wouldn't open and no one came and opened it. I sat there feeling really miserable, I barked a few times but still no one came. The rain was getting heavier and heavier.

Eventually Master opened the door and looked a little startled at me and said "What are you doing out here you silly dog" I rushed past him and shook myself right next to him, showering him in water. He dried me down with a towel and I went through to the sitting room where the other two were stretched out in front of the fire. I sat down with them, I was not at all happy.

# *Chip's rabbit*

It was a fine sunny morning and Master and Pat were taking us for a walk around the farm. Chaz and I were on leads and Chip was off. We had cleared the orchard and were heading for an area of orchard that was fenced in; which meant that we could all run free, we couldn't run away.

We were walking along a track when Chip suddenly spotted something that we hadn't. She burst into a run as a rabbit came out of the crop and ran off ahead of us with Chip in hot pursuit. We tried to join in but were held firm. Chaz became very excited. We reached a corner of the field and as we rounded it we saw Chip trotting proudly towards us with a rabbit kicking furiously in her mouth. We wanted to investigate but again we were held firm. Chaz's lead was passed to Pat and he went over to Chip. Master said "Drop it" but she was not having any of that. Master grabbed Chip's mouth and squeezed on the sides until her mouth was forced open. The rabbit dropped onto the ground and ran off apparently none the worse for its little adventure. Labradors are of course soft mouthed!

Chip was not happy at losing her prize but Master gave us all a treat, so Chaz and I didn't mind. Chip was most indignant at having to give up her catch and she did not forget for quite a while, and Master was most certainly not flavour of the month in her eyes and she avoided him as much as possible.

# *'Millie'*

On our regular walks around the farm we began to notice a strange scent on the ground, it was another dog and it was a bitch. We were picking up fresh scent on a daily basis. Eventually one morning we were to meet the new kid on the block. We had just got back from a long walk and were all stretched out on the lawn when we heard a voice at the top gate. It was Peter standing there and as we ran up to greet him we spotted a little yellow Labrador puppy who jumped up at the gate as we approached.

He brought her into the garden and we greeted her immediately. She was let off her lead and we began running around the garden with her. We soon learnt that her name was Millie. She was a ball of fun and we spent ages running and tumbling over. Several times Master and Pat shouted "Gentle you lot she is only a puppy" what ever that meant? Chaz and I were soon exhausted and collapsed in heaps on the patio. Chip and Millie continued their rough and tumble for ages. Occasionally Millie would come bounding over to us and leap all over us. It brought back memories of Chip when she was a puppy.

Millie and Chip

Eventually Peter got up to leave and Millie was placed back on her lead and they went out through the gate. Millie did not want to go and kept looking back at us as she went back to the farm house. So began a very strong friendship between the four of us, in particular between Chip and Millie. We would regularly meet on walks around the farm and Millie was a regular visitor to our garden.

On one occasion Millie was on a sleep over with us when she was a little older and she got herself into a bit of trouble. She had arrived with Jan mid afternoon with bed, food and toys. Well of course the first thing that happened was the battle of the bed as Chaz tried to take over Millie's bed. Pat was very firm with Chaz and got her off it. However as soon as Pat had disappeared Chaz reoccupied the bed and Millie lay with Chip and I.

Our food was kept in a tall bin with a firm lid on it. All three of us had tried to get into it in the past but without success, but that was until the arrival of Millie! We had been bedded down and Master and Pat had said "Good Night" and the light had gone off. We all settled down with Chaz and me laying either side of Chip and Millie on her bed at our feet. All was at peace with the world but not for long.

Millie grew restless and wanted to play but we were not interested. She began pacing around the room and found the food bin. She began sniffing it and nudging the lid. Chaz and I watched her with one eye open, little Chip was sound asleep. Millie began clawing at the lid with paw and jaw and after a considerable time the lid became detached and fell onto the floor which woke Chip up. Millie had her two front paws on the top of the bin which had been refilled that day; she was eating away quite happily. Chip could not resist the temptation and was munching away. Chaz was next up but there was not enough room for all three so Millie got down. She had eaten so much her tummy was very swollen.

I knew that this was not going to end well but the sound of munching got too much and I had to join in. We all slept well on very full stomachs, there was not much left in the bin which was lying on its side on the floor. Later in the night Millie was violently sick. Pat came down early the following morning and came into the room. She stood at the door and looked at the bin and then at us, her body language did not bode well.

She said in an angry voice "Well who did this?" but it was fairly obvious as Millie still had a swollen tummy and as we were let out she was violently sick again.

When we came back in, Pat was clearing up the mess with Master. He looked at me and Chaz and said "I don't suppose you had anything to do with this?" We all went back outside and laid low for the rest of the day. Needless to say we didn't get fed that morning!

The food bin was subsequently moved out of our room and into the shower/toilet room next door.

# *A Gang of Five*

Six months after the food bin incident Millie was staying with us when we had another arrival at Pandemonium. We had had our early morning walk with Master and Pat and were resting. Millie and Chip were playing on the lawn when a car arrived on the front gravel. I ran around to investigate with Chaz close behind me. It was Phil and Sarah and they had brought Harry. He jumped out of the car and greeted us. He ran around the back with us in pursuit and it was then that Chip and Millie spotted him. They ran up and greeted him. Millie had not met Harry before and they paid a lot of attention to each other.

When Chaz and I went indoors to our room, leaving the others running around the lawn, we found Harry's bed laid out this of course only meant one thing. Chaz was on it like a shot, until Master came in when she moved off it without being spoken to. Chaz and I went back outside and began chasing Chip and Millie who were chasing Harry. It turned into a chaotic rough and tumble as we all piled in on top of each other; only to start running around again. We were totally oblivious to the fact that Phil and Sarah had left.

That night disputes broke out as to who was sleeping on who's bed and eventually Pat and Master settled it by moving Harry and Chaz with their respective beds into the room next door, leaving me with my two young pals. Everybody slept well after the thrills and spills on the lawn.

After breakfast the following day we all went for a long walk and at the reservoir, Chaz, Millie and Harry had a good swim while Chip and I paddled. The rest of the day we hurtled around the garden chasing each other and having huge rough and tumbles. Harry had taken quite a shine to Millie and was her constant companion.

This became the pattern for the next few days, total chaos reigned. The fitness of Chaz and I was truly tested. One morning we were out on our walk as usual when a small deer appeared out of the crop and onto the track ahead of us. Harry, Millie and I were with Master and Pat had Chaz and Chip who were slightly ahead of us. Chaz and Chip saw the deer and went to chase it. They spun Pat around and she lost her footing and crashed down on to the ground with a loud thud, but she held the two leads firm. Master rushed over to her and helped her up; she was alright but was angry with Chaz and Chip. She brushed herself down and brought the two miscreants in and spoke to them very firmly. We returned home at a fairly quick pace, Chaz and Chip were very subdued until we reached the garden where the usual chaos began as our favourite game of chase began.

Chip (Asleep) Harry (At back) Chocka (In front of master) Chaz at his feet and Millie (In foreground)

Later that day Harry jumped into Pat's car and his bed and bowl were put in and he left. We sat and watched him as he left through the gate; he was watching us out of the back window. Master shut the gate. She returned a few minutes later without Harry. Later that day we were all bundled into Pat's car and were driven up to the orchard with the fence around it and Master followed in his car which was pulling a trailer. We were soon all running around the orchard playing while Pat and Master were cutting up wood with a very noisy machine which I learnt was a chain saw. We soon lay down on the grass in the shade under the trees and watched the work continue for some time. The trailer was filled with wood before we left and returned to the cottage.

That night we were all exhausted. I lay on Master's feet and Chip, Millie and Chaz were on Pat's. The following day was really hot and after a short walk we all slept on the lawn. It was even too hot for Millie to be running around. That evening we heard familiar voices approaching the top gate from the field beyond and we all ran up to the gate to investigate. It was Peter and Jan back from their holiday. Millie was really excited and gave them a huge greeting as they passed through the gate. Millie later left with them.

Life returned to normal or as normal as it could be at 'Pandemonium'.

Jake and Harry

# *Jake*

A few days after Harry's departure, Phil and Sarah arrived one evening with Beccy and Ian. Sarah was carrying a curious bundle in her arms which we all wanted to investigate. Everybody sat in the conservatory and curiosity got the better of us and we gently sniffed at the bundle and discovered that it was a baby. Everybody was looking at the baby and talking quietly. A bottle was opened with a bang which startled me and everybody stood up and chinked their glasses and said "To Jake". I had gathered by that time that Jake was the human baby's name and that he belonged to Phil and Sarah. Harry and we three had a long run around in the garden while everybody was in the conservatory talking and drinking out of glasses!

From that time on we were to see a lot more of Jake and of Harry at Pandemonium.

# Over and Out

One bright and sunny morning, after Pat and Master had eaten their breakfast on the patio, Master took us for a walk. There was a strong breeze blowing and the air was full of scent. It was my turn to be off the lead and I was ahead of Master and the other two. We had crossed the bridge over the river that ran along the bottom of our garden and had passed the bottom of Peter and Jan's garden, and were walking along a hedge with the river on the other side. I began to pick up a faint scent of a fox which as we passed a thin part of the hedge became quite strong. I dived through the hedge to investigate. As I reached the water I heard a loud commotion from behind me which startled me. I went back up to the track to investigate.

On reaching the track all I saw was Master's legs and feet disappearing through the hedge in a horizontal position! Chip and Chaz were barking excitedly and had pulled Master over and were dragging him towards the river through a thinner part of the hedge. I went back into the hedge and found Master flat out on his front shouting at my two pals who were looking very subdued. Master got to his feet and brushed himself down, he was not happy. He spoke very sternly to the other two; I returned to the path and waited.

I was put on a lead and the remainder of the walk was in silence. Master had a slight limp for the rest of the day. We kept a low profile for the remainder of the day, but that night we slept on Master and Pat's feet.

A few months later Millie was staying with us for a few days and we were out on a walk when a similar incident occurred. Master was holding Millie and Me, and Pat had Chaz and Chip. We were walking along a track on the farm with a hedge on one side and a tall crop on the other. As we reached a corner Chaz and Chip suddenly spotted something on the track and went to run after it. The severe jolt on their leads appeared to catch Pat unaware and she crashed to the ground with a loud thud, but held on to the leads. We were immediately behind her and Master rushed over and helped her up. I saw a rabbit disappearing along the track and it was obviously this that had excited the other two.

Pat brushed herself down and spoke angrily to Chaz and Chip who stood very still with their ears and tails down. We all made friends that evening.

Chaz and Chip were both very powerful dogs.

# *Playing in the Rain*

One weekend Millie was staying with us. One morning we had had a particularly long walk with Master and Pat and we settled down on the lawn although Millie wanted to play. It was hot and muggy and we were all panting heavily. Millie was full of it; she kept on jumping on us and prodding us with a paw, something I think she had learnt from Chip. During the late afternoon the sun disappeared behind a large black cloud and the sky grew darker and darker. Eventually the rain began to fall which cooled us down. Millie still wanted to play and so I got up and chased her down the garden, the others then joined in. Millie grabbed one of our toys which Chaz tried to take off her but she ran off with Chaz in hot pursuit. The rain was getting heavier and heavier as we continued the game. Chaz had managed to get the toy off of Millie and had run off with it. Millie chased after her and stole it back, Chaz was angry and barked at her.

At that point in the proceedings there was a huge flash of light in the sky which was followed almost immediately by a loud crack of thunder. The rain was now coming down in torrents but still we continued with the game despite calls from Master. Chaz and Millie were having a tug of war over another toy, but Millie had no chance, Chaz was a very powerful dog. As they pulled, Millie suddenly lost her grip on the wet and slippery grass and fell over. She was however determined to hang on to the toy and laid on the grass. Chaz tried to pull it out of her mouth but the result was that Millie finally let go. Just at that point there was another huge flash of lightening followed by a violent crack of thunder that seemed to startle Millie.

By this time we were all soaked through and Millie was covered in mud from the lawn but the game went on regardless. We ran in and out of the trees chasing each other as the rain was getting heavier and heavier until it began to hurt my eyes. Master and Pat stood at the back door and I heard the word "Treats" so we all went in just as another crack of thunder resounded over head. We were all dried off with towels which we all enjoyed. As we were dried off the lights in the cottage went out and we were plunged into darkness. Pat disappeared leaving Master to finish drying us, when he could find us! Pat reappeared shortly after with a lit candle in her hand. After we were dried we were given another treat before settling down on our beds. It was quite a while before the lights came back on.

# *A Visit to the Hospital*

Early one morning Chaz and I were bundled into the car by Pat; Chaz needed a lift as usual. As we drove out of the gate I looked out of the back window and could see little Chip's forlorn face at one of the cottage windows. After a short journey we arrived at a premises we knew well, the vets!

Pat led us in and there was no one else in the waiting room and we went straight into the vet's room. Chaz was first up on to the table with a lift from the vet and Pat. It was our annual check up. The vet trimmed Chaz's nails which she did not like at all and she made that known to everyone with the noise that she made. Soon it was all over for her and it was my turn.

I was lifted up on to the table then prodded and poked all over. I felt a sharp prick in the back of my neck. The vet then began to examine my right eye that I had been having some trouble with, a lump had developed on my eye lid and it had been very sore and weeping a lot. The vet had a long conversation with Pat and I heard the word "Operation" mentioned but of course I did not know what it meant... We were both quite relieved when we walked out of the building and back to the car. Chip gave us both a huge greeting when we got back and we played on the back lawn for ages.

That evening a large party of school children arrived at Pandemonium and we had great fun running around with them chasing our toys and having a real rough and tumble. We even managed to scrounge a few biscuits when Master and Pat were not looking! We all slept well that night.

The following morning I was bundled into the car on my own by Pat and I soon found myself back on the vet's table. I was really hungry, I had missed breakfast. I looked up at Pat when I felt a sharp jab in the back of my neck and almost immediately everything went black.

When I came to my eye was very sore and I felt groggy. I tried to fight the drowsy feeling but I was soon in a deep sleep. When I awoke much later my eye was still sore but the lump that had been bothering me had gone. At this point I discovered that I had that big lampshade around my neck which extended over my head again. I had had one of these before and I did not like it. I was in a large cage and I could see another Labrador in a cage opposite mine and she had a big collar on like mine.

A young girl came in, spoke to me in a soft gentle voice and brought me a bowl of water. I had difficulty in reaching the bowl to drink because of the collar but I soon remembered that if I pushed down hard on to it I could just reach the bowl.

Later that day a face came in that I recognised, it was Pat; was I pleased to see her! The young girl that had brought me the water and Pat helped me out of the cage and I was led out and back to the car. I received a huge greeting from Chaz and Chip when we arrived back at the cottage. Indoors I found it awkward moving around with the collar on. I kept on banging into things. The gaps that I could normally get through were proving difficult with the collar. I was given some food which Chip and Chaz tried to help me eat, but they were shut out in the garden until I had finished.

That night with some difficulty, I managed to lie down and sleep with my pals in our room, but I had a restless night with the collar on. For the next few days I slept on the lawn for most of the time. My neck was becoming sore in one particular place where the collar was chafing. It had worn away all the hair and the bare skin was raw. Pat eventually removed the collar which was a great relief for me, and I could scratch again!

Another quick trip to the vet, where my eye was examined, he seemed to be very pleased by the tone of his voice. Soon I was as right as rain and back playing with the other two as if nothing had happened. The hair on my neck soon re grew and the soreness of the eye had gone.

# *Leader of the Pack?*

As time went by and Chip grew into a fine dog and Chaz and I grew older, Chaz developed an obsession of who was leader of the pack. The pack included Master and Pat, and it was Master's authority that Chaz began to challenge. It was an issue that had never bothered me; I had been a loner all my juvenile life so the pack situation had not arisen.

A good example of Chaz's challenging of Master's authority and his position in the pack began to occur every morning after breakfast when Master was getting us ready for our walk. He would tell us to "Sit" and have our collars put on. Chip and I had no problem with that and in fact we would be sitting before he asked, but not Chaz. She would refuse to sit and would go off on a walk about around the room while Master stood and waited. Eventually she would come back over to him, in her own time and stand looking at him. He would tell her to "Sit" but she would just stand there. Eventually Master got angry with her and would say "You will sit Chaz" and pushed her rear end down and Chaz would reluctantly sit and have her collar put on.

Master would then look her straight in the eye and say "You will do as you are told dog". This became a daily routine but curiously Chaz did not do it to Pat. It was not as if Chaz was deaf, her hearing was perfect when she wanted it to be!

Another point of conflict between Master and Chaz was when Master was sitting on the patio either on his own or with company; Chaz would start barking at him. What she wanted was for him to get up and throw a toy lying right in front of her. Eventually Master would get up and walk over to her and she would grab the particular toy and run off down the garden. As soon as Master sat down again, Chaz would return to the same spot and the whole routine would start again. If Master ignored her, the barking got louder and louder. Master however did win this battle of wills for he began sending her indoors if she started playing up and she would be shut in until she had calmed down. Chaz did not like this, and came back out very subdued.

Another point of challenge was when we were running loose in the orchard with a fence around it. Master would let us run around for ages and would often sit down and watch us. Eventually he would call us in to have our leads re attached before going out through the gate. Chip and I were there and our leads were on, but Chaz had other ideas. She would grab a log that she had been chewing and would run to the other end of the orchard, where she would sit down and continue chewing her log. Master would stand there calling and calling but she ignored him. After a lot of calling from Master we all went up to the end where Chaz was but she would run off again, this made Master very angry; the tone of his voice said it all. Eventually Chaz would stroll back to us and as she did Master would often say, "In your own time Chaz, don't mind us". Master won this challenge as well, as Chaz was not allowed off her lead until she learnt to come in when called, she learnt.

When we returned from our walk either with Pat or Master we would be given a little treat once we were securely in the garden. They would however insist that we sat before receiving our treat. This was fine with Pat or if Pat and Master had taken us but when it came to Master on his own, Chaz would play him up and would refuse to sit. Master was beginning to lose patience with Chaz so the way he dealt with this was that she simply did not get a treat. She soon learnt to sit, Master won that battle.

The lawn itself became a point of challenge between Master and Chaz and it was another that she lost. Once a week during the summer Master would cut the grass with a large tractor mower, which Chip and I were not very fond of and would keep well clear of it. Chaz on the other hand saw this as an opportunity to challenge Master.

He would ride the noisy machine towards her cutting the grass as he did. As he got closer to her he would shout "Move Chaz" but she would just look at him and wag her tail and just lay there. Master would shout again with a similar response from Chaz. He would be forced to stop the tractor right in front of her and get off and as he did Chaz would move away. On the next sweep around on the mower Chaz would do it all over again but typically Master would win. He would shut her in until he had finished.

With all her confrontations with Master, she never won so I could never really understand why she did it in the first place. Eventually she stopped challenging him. I think she got the message, which was really good because it made our lives a lot better.

# *Double Trouble*

It was business as usual at Pandemonium one warm sunny morning. We had our breakfast and Pat had placed our collars on. We had heard Master leave very early. We were led out of the top gate into the field next to the garden and down to the river. It was Chip's turn to be off the lead and she was investigating scents in the field beyond the river. We walked briskly up to the bridge and crossed the river which was dry. We walked back down the other side and it was on this bank that I picked up a very strong scent of fox coming from the bank. I tried to go off and investigate but I was held firm.

Eventually we arrived at the orchard with the fence around it. We passed through the gate which Pat closed behind us. We were then let off our leads and we ran through the trees picking up one or two plums that laid on the ground, boy were they delicious. Chip even managed to grab one or two off of the lower branches, despite Pat shouting "No". Chaz and Chip were also interested in the apples that were on the ground further into the orchard, I was not quite so keen and stuck to the plums. We had a good run around before we were called back to the gate and Chip and Chaz's leads were put back on, it was my turn to run free.

As we walked away from the orchard I suddenly spotted a hare that had hopped out of the crop and onto the track ahead of us. I immediately gave chase and ignored Pat's shout for me to come back. The hare disappeared back into the crop and I followed. I could see it running down a narrow track within the crop way ahead of me, it was gaining on me with every leap. I could hear Pat blowing her whistle and Chaz barking excitedly in the distance; it was obvious that Chaz wanted to join in the chase. Suddenly the hare was gone, it had vanished. I leapt up into the air so that my head was momentarily above the crop which I had heard Master refer to as "Wheat", but I couldn't see it anywhere. I ran on and kept on leaping up and looking but the hare had gone as usual. I don't really know why we used to chase them, we could never catch them!

I came back out onto the track but I could not see Pat and my pals so I began to trot home. Along the river bank towards the bridge I suddenly picked up the fox scent again but this time I went to investigate and it was not difficult to find. The fox's scat was on the bank. I started to roll in it, initially all around my neck and collar and then all down my back and sides, oh boy was this lovely? Eventually I emerged from the river bank completely covered; I trotted home with my head held high, I smelt beautiful! When I arrived at the top gate it was closed so I sat and waited.

A short while later I saw Pat approaching along the fence from the river with my two pals. I ran to greet them but I was greeted by Pat who said "Oh no, you disgusting dog", I did not know what this meant but the tone suggested that I had done something wrong! We all passed through the gate and back into our garden. Chip and Chaz's collars were removed but Pat would not go near me. We were given our customary treat but mine was given to me at arms length and Pat said "Whooh Chocka you stink, you disgusting dog"

I was led to the hose and I knew what was coming next! Master had returned and when he saw me he said "Chocka what have you done?" I didn't know what I had done wrong but it was obvious that Pat and Master were not very happy with me. I was thoroughly hosed down and then I had shampoo applied and I was rubbed down all over until I was covered in bubbles. I was then hosed down before a second lot of shampoo was poured on to me and rubbed into my coat. This was repeated, until I was thoroughly clean. I was then dried off with a towel after I had shaken myself right next to Master who was not pleased! I did not like the hose but I did like all the attention.

I lay down on the lawn in the sun and slept for the rest of the morning as my coat dried. Later the same day 'Millie' arrived with Peter and Jan who sat on the patio with Master and Pat while we played on the lawn. Chip and I pinned Millie down after a short chase, until Chaz came wading in. Millie would leap to her feet and then we would all chase Chip who was very fast. We chased her around the flower bed in the lawn near the patio, I tried to intercept her but she leapt right over me. Eventually Millie caught her and we all piled in on her. Then it was my turn to be chased and I allowed Millie and Chip to catch me and they all bundled in. While all this was going on everybody on the patio was laughing at us. This was our usual mad play when Millie joined us.

Later that night after Millie had gone I curled up on Pat's feet. I think that what ever my misdemeanour had been earlier in the day I had been forgiven!

I slept very well that night.

# *A Good Catch*

It was a cold crisp morning and we were out across the fields with Master. We could hear the sound of guns being fired behind a hedge at the top end of the field we were in. I could see birds flying in all directions as we walked along the river some distance from the hedge.

Chip was off the lead and had already chased a fox off the river bank and she was in full hunting mode. There was a low bright sun just above the hedge.

Suddenly there was a volley of gun fire and almost immediately I saw a pheasant glide over the hedge out of the sun and down the field towards us. It was low and was simply gliding over the ground.

Chip spotted the bird and her eyes were fixed on it as it drew closer and closer towards us. Chaz had already spotted it and was barking excitedly and pulling hard on her lead. The bird did not deviate from it's course despite all the commotion from Chaz; Master was having a job holding on to her.

The bird continued gliding and was increasing in speed as it dropped down the field still aiming straight at us. I was getting excited as well as Chaz and we were almost pulling Master over. At the last moment as the bird passed over Chip's head she leapt high into the air and caught the bird in mid flight and landed on the ground with the blood stained bird held in her mouth, it had been shot but had managed to glide down the field.

Master called her in and she came and sat next to him with the now limp body of the pheasant hanging out of her mouth. Chip reluctantly gave up the bird to Master and we were all given a treat out of his pocket. Master placed the dead bird in an inside pocket of his coat and we walked back to the cottage with the long tail feathers of the bird sticking out of his coat.

The last I saw of the bird was when I watched Pat place it in the freezer!

# *Escape*

For some time we had observed the odd rabbit in the field outside the top gate and their scent was often quite strong outside the gate when we went for a walk. We had had rabbits in the garden but Pat and Master had renewed the fence in the area where they had been coming in.

One morning we had returned from our walk and we were lying on the lawn resting. It was nice and sunny and there was a strong breeze, Chip was stretched out in the shade of one of the trees. Chaz was lying next to me.

Suddenly Chip leapt to her feet and darted to the top gate, we followed close behind her. There on the grass under the hedge in the field were four rabbits busy eating the grass. Both Chaz and Chip became very excited and Chip managed to leap up and over a low part of the fence and chased after the rabbits that scattered in all directions. Chaz could not contain herself and she managed to clamber over the fence and joined in the chase. I stood and watched through the gate.

The two 'escapees' then disappeared through the hedge and out of sight. Master was out in his car and Pat was busy in the cottage. I went in and whined but Pat continued working. I went back up to the top gate but there was no sign of my pals. I ran around to the front as I had heard a commotion coming from the direction of the road. I looked through the front gate and could see Jan holding on to Chip by the scruff of her neck and both were walking towards the gate. At that point Pat appeared at the front door and shouted to me "What is it Chocka?" and approached me. She then caught sight of Jan and Chip approaching. She opened the gate and spoke to Jan, Chip skulked through the gate and Pat said to her in an angry voice "Where have you been?" Chip walked off with her tail between her legs and disappeared into the cottage.

Jan then left and Pat ran around the back of the cottage and up to the top gate, there was no sign of Chaz. She went back to the cottage and returned with a lead. I watched as she went out into the field and walked along the high hedge calling "Chaz". Eventually she appeared through the hedge and approached Pat looking very guilty. Her lead was put back on and she was led back through the gate which was firmly closed. Chaz disappeared into the cottage and lay down with her daughter.

Pat repaired the fence and raised the height of the wire; the breach in the defences was blocked!

# *Plums!*

It was the time of the year when the fruit in the orchard tasted beautiful. We spent a lot of time in the fenced off orchard where Chaz and Chip filled themselves on the juicy plums on the ground. I had one or two but they ate a lot more. I was more interested in the apples which I really enjoyed.

One morning we left the cottage with Master and Pat and headed towards the orchard. Pat was carrying an empty basket. On reaching the orchard, Pat went and closed the gate, leaving us outside with Master who had us all on leads. Chaz and Chip got quite excited as we watched Pat through the wire as she filled the basket with plums. Eventually Pat re emerged through the gate with the basket full of plums. Master let me off my lead and I began to follow Pat. Master had Chaz on her lead and Pat had Chip.

Pat was carrying the basket in her hand down by her side.

I was walking alongside Master when Chaz crept forward to Pat and very gently stole a plum out of the

Thief!

Getting Greedy

basket which was just the right height for her to reach it. Neither Pat or Master or Chip saw it. Chaz ate it as we walked. She crept forward and stole another and another until Pat suddenly spotted her and told her off. As we walked on Chaz tried again but Master pulled her back with a sharp jerk.

We had walked on quite a way when Pat stopped to untangle Chip's lead that had got twisted and knotted. Chaz seized the opportunity and lunged at the basket, which she hit so hard that a few of the plums spilled out on to the ground. I kept out of the way as I knew this was not going to end well. Chip and her Mum made quick work of them, despite shouts from Master and Pat, and a sharp jerk on Chaz's lead. Chip swept up the last plum as Pat tried to reach down and gather it up. She had a serious telling off from Pat. During the remainder of the walk home Pat held the basket out of reach of the thieves and Master dropped right back so that Chaz could not reach Pat even with the lead fully extended.

I went off and investigated some interesting scents on the side of the track under the hedge. There were shallow holes dug into the grass and soil and these were filled with dark droppings, the scent that they gave off was really interesting. Master called me in just as I was about to roll in it. He told me that they were "Badger latrines" whatever they were I didn't know but they were certainly interesting, especially as they were full of plum stones, obviously badgers like plums!!

A few days later we were out across the fields again with Master and Pat who were both carrying buckets. We stopped in front of a hedge and they began picking small dark berries off the hedge and placed them into the buckets. Master dropped one of these berries onto the ground and I picked it up and bit into it but immediately spat it out, it tasted very bitter and horrible. Master told me that they were "Sloes"; all I knew was that sloes did not taste nice. It was a long time till I could get rid of the taste in my mouth.

Further around the next hedge we met up with Peter and Millie and we greeted each other. Millie went off across the stubble field playing with Chip as Master, Pat and Peter talked. Pat had placed her bucket on to the ground and I watched Chaz as she reached into the bucket to steal one. I saw her bite into one and then screwed up her face and spat it out with a disgusted look on her face. Pat turned to her and laughed and said "Serves you right" and everyone started laughing. She didn't try to steal any more!

# *Harry's amorous advances*

One afternoon all three of us were asleep on our beds in our room when we heard a car arrive on the gravel out the front. We ran around to investigate. Phil, Sarah and Jake had arrived and they'd brought Harry who leapt out of the back of the car. We greeted him enthusiastically and all four of us ran around the garden chasing each other.

Phil and Master stood on the lawn throwing our toys for us to catch, but Harry got them every time. Phil and Master then disappeared into the cottage leaving us all on the lawn. I could see Master with young Jake on his lap in the conservatory with the others.

Harry went off and investigated all around the garden while we sat and watched him. Eventually he returned to us and he suddenly turned his attentions towards me. He sidled up to me and tried to put his paw on my back but I was not interested and rolled on to my back. When I stood up, he tried to put his front paw across my back again so I snapped at him and ran off, but he pursued me to the bottom of the garden where he tried it again, so I rolled on to my back and snapped at him, but he would not take no for an answer.

I ran back up to the top of the lawn where Chaz and Chip were sitting watching. Harry followed me but on reaching the others he turned his attentions to Chaz, but she sent him away with a loud bark and snap, he leapt out of the way as she chased him away. He then came back to me and tried it on again so I sent him off with the same treatment that he got from Chaz, he didn't like that and returned very cautiously; he didn't try it on again.

We all lay down on the lawn close to one another and licked each other. Later Harry was placed back into his car and he left.

# *Burglars beware dogs about!*

Master and Pat had taken us for a long early morning walk and we were all sound asleep on the lawn when Pat called us in and gave us a treat. She then locked the back door top and bottom before leaving with Master. We heard the front door slam shut, soon after Master's car leaving the front yard and the gate slammed shut.

We went to sleep but were awoken by the sound of footsteps on the gravel out the front of the cottage. I heard the door bell ring and Chaz began barking. Soon after we saw a man's face at the window and Chip leapt up at the window barking loudly in her deep voice. I then realised that there was another man standing nearby. They then disappeared and we heard them moving around the back of the cottage.

We ran to the back door as a face appeared at the small window in the back door. We all jumped up at the door barking as we heard the men trying to open the door with the handle. We heard the men moving away across the gravel and heard a loud banging coming from the conservatory. We ran through to the conservatory and saw the men at the door, they appeared to be trying to force the doors open. We flew at the glass barking aggressively which caused the men to jump back.

They quickly moved back to the back door and we raced through to the door as they began banging hard on the door. I leapt up at the window and barked with the others as the men moved away again. We ran back to the conservatory where the men had returned to. They were standing at the door and were holding a large block of concrete between them and it was obvious to me that they were about to throw it through the glass. We were barking at the top of our voices.

As the men began to swing the block towards the glass, all three of us moved back. At that point the men both looked all around them and appeared to spot a person walking along the river at the bottom of the garden, it was Peter and Millie. They dropped the block and ran off around the front of the cottage. We ran through to the kitchen and above our barking I could hear footsteps on the front gravel then fade away.

We couldn't settle but kept on patrolling around the cottage to see if the men had returned but they had gone. We had done our job!

Eventually Master and Pat returned totally unaware of the excitement we had experienced and lit the fire. We curled up in front of the fire and slept deeply.

The following morning Pat found the concrete block lying on the gravel outside the conservatory doors, I don't think they ever knew how it got there, but we did!

# *Bar B Q*

Pat came down early one morning as a result of Chaz's barking as dawn broke, her body language spoke volumes. We had our breakfast and Pat sat with us for quite a while till Master appeared. He put our collars and leads on and we were off across the fields, there were some interesting scents on the ground. Chip tried to go after a rabbit that ran off through the orchard but Master held her firm. We met up with Peter and Millie who gave us all a boisterous greeting before we walked on. Eventually we were back at the cottage and after our customary treat at the gate after our collars were removed we went and lay down on the lawn.

Master spent some time dragging a large barrel on wheels out of the garage and around on to the patio where he proceeded to clean it. I had heard Master and Pat refer to this as the "Bar B Q" whatever that meant, but all I knew was that there was some delicious food that came out of it. Much later I saw smoke billowing out of the bar b q and when Master went over to it and opened the lid he all but disappeared in a cloud of smoke.

Peter and Jan arrived later, we looked around for Millie but she wasn't with them.

Soon after Phil, Sarah, Jake and Harry arrived; we had a game of chase around the garden with Harry until we all collapsed on the lawn. Beccy and Ian then arrived. Ian spent some time throwing a ball for us, which Harry invariably caught. While all this was going on Master began cooking on the Bar B Q... Chaz and I sneaked away from the games and crept over to a table close to Master, there were some very interesting scents coming from the table, especially after the first plate of cooked sausages were put down on the table. We slowly crept up to the table as there was no one watching, Master had his back to us. We leaned over the table and managed to sneak a sausage each. We slipped away holding the very hot sausage in our mouths and went down to the bottom of the lawn where we both laid down and ate our stolen property. It was still very hot but boy did it taste nice.

We licked our lips as we went back to the table for more but the table was empty. Everyone was sitting at tables on the patio eating and talking. We went on the scrounge visiting each person in turn until Master told us off so we returned to the lawn where Harry and Chip were sound asleep.

After the food had been eaten, everybody sat around talking for quite a while until Phil and Sarah got up and started throwing a ball for us. Master was walking around the garden with a pram with Jake sound asleep inside. I kept checking on him but he didn't wake once as Master made several circuits.

As the sun began to set everybody began to leave. Jake was placed on the back seat of a car in his pram and Harry jumped in the back and Phil and Sarah left, followed soon after by Beccy, Ian, Peter and Jan. Master and Pat spent some time clearing up outside and inside, while Chaz, Chip and I hoovered up any scraps on the patio where everybody had been sitting, there was not a lot! Eventually Master and Pat sat down in the sitting room and Chaz, Chip and I joined them... I settled down on Master's feet after he had made a fuss of all three of us. As I settled down he looked down at me and said with a smile "I hope you enjoyed your sausages!" but of course I didn't know what he meant!

We all slept very well that night.

# *Pippa*

Early one morning we were taken for a long and brisk walk by Master in the rain. On reaching the big field near the reservoir, I saw Millie on the far side of the field and she was racing towards us leaving Peter far behind. On reaching us she crashed into Master, almost knocking him off of his feet. She then chased and played with Chip who was off her lead. Eventually Peter arrived and he and Master spoke for some time before Millie was placed back on her lead and they left.

On reaching the fenced orchard, we were let off our leads. Chip ran off and began eating the apples on the ground. Chaz found a log and began chewing it between eating apples. I walked along by Master's side. The rain had stopped and a breeze had got up. On reaching the far end, Master sat down and I sat on his feet.

Eventually Master stood up and our leads were re attached and we left the orchard. We walked around the big field, in one corner we all picked up a strong scent of a fox but we were not allowed to go off and investigate.

As we walked along the fence with the line of trees on the other side in our garden, I saw another Labrador running around on our territory. All three of us began to pull Master up to the top gate. We met the new dog at the gate and we soon learnt that her name was 'Pippa'. After our leads were removed we ran off and played, although she appeared a little nervous of us. We had met her before but it was a long time ago. Mike was standing on the patio; his scent on previous visits had indicated that he was related to Pat. Master, Pat and Mike disappeared into the conservatory and sat down. We ran around the garden and had a good rough and tumble with Pippa.

Much later we were shut into our room and I heard Mike's vehicle leave the front drive, Pippa was sitting with us. She was still very nervous but I suppose it was not surprising with us lot at 'Pandemonium'. As it transpired Pippa was to stay with us for a long time.

Pippa spent a very disturbed first night, whimpering and pacing up and down in our room. For once Chaz did not challenge Pippa for her bed as she had done for Harry's bed. It may be that Pippa's bed was not as comfortable as hers. The following morning Chaz began barking as dawn broke and Pippa joined her, Pat came in and by the tone of her voice she was not amused. We were fed and there was a little dispute over our feeding bowls, Chaz and I both went for Pippa's bowl and Pat had to step in, firmly. Afterwards, we were let out into the garden and we had a good romp with Pippa. We all collapsed on the lawn and Chip licked Pippa's face, they are becoming good friends.

Master and Pat had their breakfast in the conservatory. We went in and pestered the two of them as we wanted to go for a walk. After a lot of barking from Chaz they eventually gave in and our collars and leads were put on and we were off. Although they were on their leads, Chip and Pippa were still able to play. We had a long walk and collapsed in our beds when we got back.

Pippa (left Millie (Right)

Later that morning I heard a familiar whining at the top gate, it was Millie. We all ran up to the gate and greeted her when she came in. Peter followed shortly after and he gave us all a treat before disappearing into the conservatory. Pippa and Millie hurtled around the garden with Chip, while Chaz and I sat and watched. Chaz was barking at them, I don't really know why she did this but it was a regular habit which she also did when Chip and I were playing.

Pippa ran through one of the flower beds which we knew was a big 'No'. Pat came racing out and shouted at Pippa as she was about to run back through the bed, she ran off down the lawn. Pat went back into the conservatory. We continued to watch them as the three youngsters chased around, but this came to an abrupt end. All three were racing up the garden and were heading straight for the pond.

From Left to Right
Chaz, Chip, Millie, Chocka, Pippa.

On and on they came and by the time they reached the pond they were at full speed. Pippa was in the lead, being chased by Millie and with Chip close behind. On reaching the pond and without a break in her stride, Pippa took an almighty leap and flew through the air for what seemed to be an age before crashing into the middle of the pond with a huge splash. Millie followed, creating a second huge splash. I knew that this was not going to end well as Pat and Master come racing out. The body language said it all, Master shouted at the two who were enjoying swimming around in the pond amongst the fish.

They climbed sheepishly out of the water dripping. They shook themselves and skulked off with ears down and their tails between their legs. Chip, Chaz and I knew that the pond was a definite 'No no', Pippa and Millie had also learnt. Peter and Millie left shortly after.

Pippa soon settled into the routine and established her position in our pack. She would wake up with Chaz early in the morning and join her in the 'Dawn choruses' until either Master or Pat came down and fed us, it was usually Pat. Pippa and Chip got on very well and played all day. Pippa's initial nervousness was rapidly disappearing.

A few days after the pond incident, we all woke early and went for a long walk with Master and Pat. Soon after we returned, Chip became unwell. She was violently sick all day. Master and Pat were working in the garden all day and kept an eye on her. We all sat with Pat as she worked in the long flower bed. Chip kept going off and vomiting, she was thoroughly miserable and not herself at all.

As darkness fell, Master and Pat sat on the patio and talked, I sat near them. Pippa jumped up on to Master's lap with her front paws and she made a real fuss of him. He gave her a big hug and made a fuss of her. I felt a little jealous; I had never felt that before when he made a fuss of Chip or Chaz, it was a strange feeling. It did not last long as he gave me a big hug and stroked my tummy which I always loved. Later that evening Pippa attempted to climb up on Pat's lap and was quite persistent. I did not like this, jealousy again. I sidled in and pushed Pippa out of the way, Pat and Master laughed, I didn't understand why?

Although Chaz and Chip were not interested in Pippa's bed, I was, it was quite comfortable, so I moved in. Pippa did not mind, she slept with the others; but Master and Pat did, I was chased out more than once. As soon as they had gone I was back in the big bed and going off to sleep. On one occasion I was stretched in the bed sound asleep when

Master came in. He shouted at me, although I did not understand exactly what he was saying, the tone said it all and I did understand the words "get out" and "No". I got the message and didn't go back in again.

After our early morning walk we were playing in the garden when I heard a whining at the top gate, it was Millie. We all raced up and greeted her as Pat let her in. Peter arrived a few minutes later. We played for ages; Peter left later leaving Millie with us. Master was working in the nature reserve at the end of the garden which was a 'No Go' area for us.

Later in the day Master came out of the nature reserve and closed the gate behind him. He was walking up the lawn towards the patio and we were all following him. Suddenly I heard a whoosh of wings behind me and turned to see a pheasant land on the grass at the bottom of the lawn and it ran towards the flower bed and disappeared into the undergrowth. Chip had also seen it and ran down the garden with Millie and Pippa behind her. She ran into the flower bed and reappeared moments later with the pheasant in her mouth. She proudly ran up to Master with the other two sniffing at the bird. Master tried to take the bird from her but she was a little reluctant to give it up but eventually he managed to prize it from her mouth.

Master walked back to the cottage with the bird. He disappeared in through the back door and that was the last we saw of the bird although when we did eventually go in there were plenty of feathers on the kitchen floor. Peter later collected Millie who was quite exhausted with all the excitement. As usual he gave us all a treat.

Another chaotic day started with the arrival of Peter and Millie just after we had returned from our walk. We had a frantic run around the garden while Peter, Pat and Master went into the conservatory. Eventually Chaz and I went and laid down in our beds, leaving the youngsters to it. Later Peter left via the top gate, Millie was left with us. Soon after Master and Pat came out on to the lawn, Master had his silver coloured box hanging around his neck, I had heard him refer to it before as his "Camera". Pat tried to get us all to sit in front of Master and to achieve this we were all given treats which were nice. Despite this Millie and Pippa did not want to sit still at all; mind you, I for one didn't mind as it meant that we had more treats.

Pat returned to working in her flower bed and Master simply wandered around the garden. Pippa and Millie grew more and more boisterous and on one occasion Chaz had just got to her feet after having a lay down on the lawn, when Pippa crashed into her shoulder with a loud crash. Chaz gave out a loud yelp and walked off a short distance before sitting down. Almost immediately Millie was running fast after Pippa when she collided head on into Chaz's head, another loud yelp and she had had enough, rather shaken she disappeared indoors.

Master went in to check on her. Millie, Chip and Pippa continued their boisterous games while Chaz and I were safely out of the action, Millie and Pippa ganged up on Chip who soon joined us panting heavily and we laid with Chaz, who I think was a little shaken after the collisions. As darkness fell Master placed Millie back on to her lead and they left via the top gate and Master returned shortly after, minus Millie. We all slept very well that night. Chaz was none the worse for wear after her knocks.

One lunch time we heard a car arrive on the front drive and we all ran around to investigate. It was Phil and Sarah and Jake. After the gate was closed, Harry was let out of the back of the car. He greeted us all excitedly and we all ran around the back and a frantic game of chase ensued all around the garden while Phil and Sarah who was holding Jake went into the conservatory.

Chaz and I had soon had enough of all this running around and stretched out on the lawn in the sun. Harry had taken a real fancy to Pippa and he followed her around all afternoon but she was not at all interested, she had had her operation! As darkness fell, Phil, Sarah, Harry and Jake left and life at Pandemonium returned to some semblance of normality. The fire was lit and we all slept in front of it; I was on Master's feet. Pippa went into a really deep sleep and began snoring loudly and was dreaming, was it Harry I wonder!

Soon after Harry's visit Gina and Stuart arrived; their arrival normally meant that Master and Pat were going away. Gina and Stuart have been regular visitors over the years to look after us. This visit was to be no different as we saw some cases piled up at the front door of the cottage the following morning. Later that same morning Millie arrived and immediately began chasing around the garden with Pippa and Chip. Chaz and I sat and watched the youngsters. Soon after Millie's arrival we heard a car leaving the front yard, Master and Pat had gone.

The walk the following morning was interesting, we were taken up to the reservoir where Gina and Stuart sat on a seat overlooking the water, the sun was shining and there was a gentle breeze. They sat there patiently for quite a while but eventually, Pippa and Millie became restless and began pulling on their leads which forced Gina and Stuart to walk on and we walked around the big field with the fenced in orchard before we returned home. That was the pattern of our days until Master and Pat returned home. We greeted them as they got out of their car and shortly after Peter and Jan called in and collected Millie.

A few days later Pat left the cottage early one morning in her car, I heard it leaving the drive. Master gave us our usual breakfast treats before we went out onto the lawn. A short while later Millie arrived at the top gate with Peter who spoke briefly to Master before leaving. Millie and Pippa were busy playing at the bottom of the garden and didn't see him leave. Chip went and joined in the chase while Chaz and I sat close together and watched.

Master disappeared indoors and soon after he had gone Pippa ran full pelt up the lawn being chased by Millie. On reaching the pond Pippa leapt in again, and was immediately followed by Millie. They swam around for a while before climbing out. The water cascaded over the patio as they shook their coats. I crept indoors and Master let me into the kitchen and then let me follow him upstairs where he was working in the room where a cot and high chair were. He was clearing out a number of boxes and I laid down and watched him; he was talking to me all the time, but I didn't understand a word he was saying except I heard the name "Jake" mentioned a number of times, till I fell asleep.

I later rejoined the others who were still running around, although Chip was worn out and was asleep on the bed. Eventually Pat returned and we all ran out and greeted her. Master lit the fire as darkness fell. We all went through and settled down in front of the fire. As we went through to the fire somebody was sick on the carpet; I do not know who it was but the tone of Master's voice indicated that he was not happy! Later that evening Peter and Jan collected Millie and she left, leaving us all exhausted, she certainly does have a lot of energy!

On another occasion Pippa and I were playing a game of tug of war with one of our rubber toys. We were in the conservatory which had a tiled floor so we could not get a grip with our paws. With us both holding on tight to the toy I would pull on it and Pippa would slide across the floor and as soon as I stopped, Pippa would pull me along the floor, backwards and forwards we went for ages. Master and Pat sat laughing at us.

As Christmas rapidly approached, the decorations appeared in the cottage and the strange lights appeared in the windows. The tree was outside the conservatory waiting to be brought in.

One cold morning, we went outside after breakfast to snow falling. After Master and Pat had eaten their breakfast in the conservatory, we took them for a walk. Soon after we returned, Peter and Millie arrived and Pippa and Millie greeted each other and began racing around the garden while Pat, Master and Peter sat in the conservatory. Chaz was sound asleep in her bed, Chip and I sat on the patio watching the two youngsters racing around on the lawn.

Peter and Millie eventually left and we all curled up in bed and the back door was shut. A little while later we heard a car arrive on the gravel in the front drive. Pippa jumped up at the kitchen window and became very excited. Pat went outside and returned shortly after with Pippa's Master Mike. Pippa greeted him enthusiastically, she was overjoyed to see him after so long. She sat at his feet in the conservatory while he spoke to Master and Pat during lunch.

Later that afternoon Mike and Pippa left, Chip and I jumped up at the window and saw Pippa's face at the rear window of the vehicle as it left. After the gate was closed we were let out and we ran around to the front. Pippa's seven week holiday with us had come to an end and I for one was going to miss her.

The day after Pippa left, we awoke to deep snow which was great fun. All of us had a great time running around in it, dashing through the trees, knocking the snow off the branches on to us, there were some interesting scents on the snow, including a fox that had visited our garden overnight. The snow dazzled us as we went for a walk with Pat and Master. I found the strong scent of deer but I was on a lead and I didn't get a chance to investigate the scent.

The following day we discovered that more snow had fallen overnight and on our walk with Master we found that it was quite deep in places. The snow dazzled us in the bright sun light. I was off the lead and the other two were walking Master! There were some interesting scents around, including a rabbit that I startled on the track leading to the fenced in orchard. I gave chase and soon disappeared through the hedge. As I cleared the ditch the other side I startled a solitary deer that was standing in the snow further along the hedge.

I forgot about the rabbit and went after the deer which was a lot more fun. I was soon struggling through the deep snow and the deer was disappearing in the distance. I could hear Master whistling and calling my name in the distance. The deep snow took its toll on me and I was soon exhausted.

I struggled over the ditch which was full of snow and back through the hedge. Master and the other two were nearby; as I approached Master I sensed that he was not very happy with me but he didn't say anything but I was put on a lead for the rest of the walk!

More snow fell over the next few days and it remained till after Christmas, getting deeper and deeper all the time and it was very cold, a factor that made my nose run constantly. There were the usual comings and goings over the Christmas period and we met up with some old friends, including Beth and Daisy who stayed with us one night. We got some nice presents from underneath the tree in the conservatory, some nice toys. After Christmas the snow lasted for quite a long time before melting away. Life returned to some form of normality, or as normal as it could be at 'Pandemonium'

Chocka: "I'm sure my present is in here"

# *Life goes on*

Since the traumas of my early life on the streets of Saffron Walden, Pat and Master have given me a wonderful home and life with Chaz and more recently Chip and our good friends Millie, Brodie, Pippa and Harry, Beth and Daisy. I have met lots of interesting people and dogs on my journey through life.

Late one afternoon, Master was working on some logs outside the top gate and was sitting with a cup in his hand, looking out across the valley, as the sun was setting. He had left the top gate slightly open so I crept out and joined him. I sat between his legs and laid my head on his knee and looked up at him, we were good pals.

It has taken me a long time to tell Master my story, and with a lot of patience on both our parts we have completed it. I hope you have enjoyed it as much as Master and I have enjoyed writing it.

Chip is now 3 years old and Millie just a year. Chaz and I plod on as the 'old ladies' of the pack. Life is always unpredictable at 'Pandemonium'

I have been very lucky and I know it!

Life goes on and the story continues.

Master and Chocka

Chocka

Chocka Chaz and Chip

As a footnote to my story, Master has asked me to say that after reading this story, the reader may be under the impression that myself along with all my friends were totally out of control but be assured that we were under control for 99.9% of the time!

Also available from the same author

# THE WILDLIFE MAN

From a very young age, 'The Wildlife Man' loved and held a fascination with animals.
This is the story of how his passion for wildlife, originally a hobby, became first a part of his job as a police officer, then his full-time occupation and his life.
He is respected and admired for his work to this day. This is a heartfelt book, and the author's passion and appreciation for wildlife and nature is infectious.

Published by Upfront Publishing, 2002
ISBN 978-184426-026-3

Also available from the same author

# RUNNING WILD

'Running Wild' is the story of a fox called Tarn who lived on the author's farm in the early 1950s, with steam trains on the LMS railway line, narrow boats trading on the Grand Union canal and 3,000 free-range chickens all on the farm.
Although this is a fictional story, some of the events described in the tale did occur and are seen through the eyes of Tarn.

Published by Upfront Publishing, 2005
ISBN 978-184426-327-4

Also available from the same author

# CASSIE

This is an amusing story told by Cassie of her many adventures and experiences during her very active life, including assisting her Master in his role as a Village Bobby

Published by Upfront Publishing, 2006
ISBN 978-184426-395-0

Also available from the same author

# Jack of all Trades

The contents of this book are a few amusing incidents that happened to the author during his time as a rural 'Bobby' and Wildlife Crime Officer with Essex Police with whom he served for 32 years.

During his service many varied incidents, both sad and amusing, ocurred which emphasises how a policeman really is a 'Jack of All Trades.

Published by Fastprint Publishing, 2009
ISBN: 978-184426-538-1